My Journey to Meet Jane Goodall

My Journey to Meet
Jane Goodall

Gregg Chavaria

ABOOKS
Alive Book Publishing

My Journey to Meet Jane Goodall
Copyright © 2016 by Gregg Chavaria

Additional copies may be ordered from the publisher for educational,
business, promotional or premium use.
For information, contact ALIVE Book Publishing
at: alivebookpublishing.com, or call (925) 837-7303.

Book Design by Alex Johnson
Dedication Page Illustration by Richard Graff

ISBN 13
978-1-63132-009-5

ISBN 10
1631320092

Library of Congress Control Number: 2015935105

Library of Congress Cataloging-in-Publication Data
is available upon request.

First Edition

Published in the United States of America by
ALIVE Book Publishing and ALIVE Publishing Group,
imprints of Advanced Publishing LLC
3200 A Danville Blvd., Suite 204, Alamo, California 94507
alivebookpublishing.com

PRINTED IN THE UNITED STATES OF AMERICA

10 9 8 7 6 5 4 3 2 1

In Memory of our dear friend, Pete.

This book is dedicated to my sweetheart,
Stacey
for all her encouragement.

Special thanks to my father
for his guidance and wisdom.

Introduction

Twenty years from now you will be more disappointed by the things you didn't do than by the ones you did do. So throw off the bowlines, sail away from the safe harbor. Catch the trade winds in your sails. Explore. Dream. Discover.   ~ H. Jackson Brown Jr.

This is a fictionalized account of a true travel tale that follows a discouraged young journalist from California to war-torn Croatia. There he meets and is smitten by a young woman who leads him to Africa: Nairobi Kenya; the Savannah Grasslands; Dar es Salaam, Tanzania and the Gombe National Reserve, where they live and work briefly with the legendary Dr. Jane Goodall. Together they embark on a journey through the great continent and into each other's hearts.

PART I

Chapter One

"The lean years had grown into a decade or more, and it showed on the man's face like so many wrinkles on a dried prune," explained the weary journalist as he leaned back and took a long, final drag from his cigarette, as if he needed the calming effects of the smoke before he continued his tale. As the smoke slowly exited his lungs, he dropped the cigarette butt on the wooden floor of the quiet, dimly lit bar, extinguishing it under the weight of his worn leather boot, and continued. "He was physically worn out. It was the kind of tired that a hot bath and a year's worth of sleep could help, but not cure. This was exhaustion of the soul. The constant attack on his senses had taken its toll, and he appeared as if he had reached a breaking point. His strength had fled his being a long time ago after years of fighting. He was broken, finished, kaput. I had never seen a broken man nor quite understood the term, but when I saw him, I knew one was standing before me. Last night was the final straw as nameless, faceless shells launched by Serbian guns slammed into his home, killing his wife and three children. I watched as he walked back through the doorway into the smoldering pile of rubble that was once a flourishing family dwelling. His family now lay dead beneath stone, earth, and debris as he cried and chanted what sounded like prayers over their lifeless remains. Suddenly, a single shot ripped through the cold, still air. I rushed through the doorway, but it was too late. All the color was leaving his body, and it spilled forth from a gaping hole in the back of his head onto the already saturated ground. It almost didn't look real as the blood collected in a neat pool. Warmth escaped from the wound and rose upward in the morning air. His body grew cooler with every passing second. His eyes were open, staring at me. I felt a chill develop at my feet and travel upward through my body as I carefully closed his eyes."

The journalist's lips were trembling and his face grew pale, as if the dead man were right there in front of him.

"After a moment of silence, numbness replaced the chill, and I spoke to his lifeless body. I prayed for him as the sting of warm tears flowed over my cheeks and down my neck. Burying this man would help put the soul to rest. Whether it was my soul or his that was being put to rest was of no importance." He paused and looked up at those gathered around the small pub table, hoping to find validation in the blank faces that stared back at him, but there was only silence. He lowered his head and carried on. "Using a shallow bomb crater, I placed the body, head first, into the grave and then used a metal bowl to shovel the earth on top of him. I will never forget the sound of earth hitting human flesh. To mark his grave, I used wood splintered from the shelling. That evening my journal entry was brief: Today, I witnessed a man take his life. I buried him."

Hearing the journalist's tale in a pub was my introduction to Zagreb, the capital of Croatia, a part of the former Yugoslavia and a country embroiled in war. It was no baptism by fire, but this man's story was permanently seared into my memory. From the day I arrived at Zagreb's international airport, the presence of war manifested itself immediately. Only one civilian flight per day was permitted; the rest of the arrivals were reserved for United Nations troops and supplies. The airport had become a staging ground for the U.N. Protective Force (UNPRFO): rows of U.N. trucks, personnel carriers, and armor cluttered the tarmac, along with clusters of marching "blue helmets"—a slang phrase for U.N. peacekeeping soldiers. There

I was, fresh out of U.C. Berkeley, right in the middle of real life, "the one thing college will not prepare you for," everyone had warned me. They were right. It didn't, but then again, nothing really prepares one to face human existence in its most ruthless state. But this place, Croatia, although chaotic and surrounded by death, held an attraction for me—it provided the perfect atmosphere for hiding out. Here, nothing seemed to matter except staying alive. Who you were, what you did, meant nothing because in war you're either a survivor or a victim.

I guess that was exactly why I had come here, to get away and figure out what to do with my life. It all started when I received a rejection letter from the Harvard Law School admissions office, notifying me I had been "denied entrance" to the class of 1993. For as long as I could remember, I had planned to be an attorney, but not getting into law school buried that dream. My life was thrown into a tumultuous sea of confusion and uncertainty. My parents kept asking me, "What are you going to do now?" Hell, I didn't have the faintest glint of an idea.

The Croatia trip came on the heels of the rejection letter and provided me with an ideal way to escape the nightly parental inquisition and having to make any decisions about my immediate future. For the moment, I filled my days writing a weekly column called "Youth in Politics" for a local newspaper. Through my writing, I labored to lessen the overwhelming isolation and disenfranchisement from the political process that many young people experience. The youths I spoke with said they believed the political process worked for older citizens, people like their parents and grandparents, but not for the young. Personally, I could not fault their feelings. My generation was the product of high divorce rates, two parents working, and intense advertising campaigns to turn us into consuming automatons. Terms like "latchkey kid" typified our family lives, while we in "Generation X" painfully stated our worth to society. Immersed in this atmosphere, who could blame us for our

apathy? As a product of this generation, I knew firsthand the po-
tential that lay beneath the veneer of grunge fashion, video
screens, excessive soft drink consumption, and acne, and as a reporter capturing the stories of this generation, I tried to unveil
it.

Wanting to do something similar in Zagreb, I had volunteered with a group called Earth Train, a nonprofit organization
based in Orinda, California, that promoted youth awareness for
environmental, political, and social issues throughout the world.
Its members, ranging in age from thirteen to more than seventy,
were dedicated to making the world a better place. They pur-
sued this goal by conducting community cleanups and informa-
tional seminars at local high schools, bringing attention to timely
topics, including the impact of pollution on the environment,
impoverished inner-city youth, and the importance of young
people being politically active. Their latest venture had led them
to Zagreb in an effort to work with the hundreds, if not thousands, of refugee children now living in camps around the capital city. Together they prepared seminars for youth
empowerment, initiated plans to develop a refugee youth center,
and organized a concert in a city park. The concert was a welcome respite from the day-to-day doldrums of life as a young
refugee. I traveled through Zagreb recording my experiences
with Earth Trainers and refugee children, capturing some of
their stories on paper and sharing them.

Suddenly, a voice coming from the other end of the bar interrupted my thoughts. It was the only female voice in a sea of
male voices in that small place, which had probably been intended for storage rather than the full-fledged watering hole it
had become. The ceiling was low, and the smell of stale beer and
cheese pizza (the only food served in the establishment) permeated the air. A blanket of smoke danced heavily above my head.

Any woman who could manage to get a word in edgewise
around this joint was definitely worth getting a closer look at.

Without being able to see her, I let her voice lead me. A thick crowd of patrons huddled around the room, preferring the warmth of cigarettes and room-temperature beers to the chilly air outside. Getting past them was like slipping through a door barely ajar. I did my best to squeeze through with little disturbance and finally came within a few yards of the woman whose voice I'd heard. The bulbs overhead were covered with a brownish film of age and cast a shadow, making it difficult to get a good look at this mystery woman. The only things that I could see clearly were that she was standing, she was tall—close to six feet—and her long, curly, dirty blonde hair had a wild sensuality about it.

She was heavily engaged in a debate, so I decided to postpone any further advance and remained wedged between a heavyset guy and a wooden beam supporting the roof. The discussion was, appropriately, over foreign policy—specifically, what the U.S. role should be in bringing this bloody regional conflict to an end. The guy was arguing that for nearly nine hundred years the residents of this region have hated each other. "Despite the fact that they are living together and have even married into each other's families, religion runs like a tainted sword through the hearts of these people, dooming them to hate one another for eternity," the heavyset patron explained.

The mystery woman retorted, "If it is possible to live together and even intermarry, couldn't one logically conclude that some lasting peace is not entirely impossible?"

"Ah, an optimist," I said to myself, smiling.

The man at the bar laughed loudly and shouted, "Vendetta!" He continued, "The vendetta continues to this day and will be carried on by the next generation. Today it appears that the Serbs are the bad guys for slaughtering the Croats, but the last time these two peoples fought each other this viciously, it was the Croats persecuting the Serbs, using the Nazis during World War II to settle the score regarding long-standing religious hatreds. Many Serbs justify their actions as avenging the deaths of generations past. This current conflict will provide fodder for future generations of Croats to avenge more deaths. The vendetta mentality." He finished, shaking his head.

"So violence begets violence until the innocent are killed alongside the guilty," she snapped with a sarcastic bite as she smiled. "So what you're saying is that there is nothing we can do to change how things are, since we are, in a sense, doomed by history? Is this what you are telling me?" He swallowed hard and realized there was fire in this woman's soul. "You know, sir, I appreciate your history lesson, and although you may be correct with your chronological sequencing, my opinion of history is entirely different from yours. See, I view history not as something we are doomed to repeat, but something used to learn, to enlighten, assisting us to never make the same mistakes. I agree that knowing what occurred in the past is important, but I, unlike you, in no way believe that life can be reduced to some redundant loop. Is that really how you view life? Because if the Serbs and Croats are destined, as you say, to be mortal enemies for eternity, then by this logic, the same is true for all of us and whatever our predestined future might be. How does one raise a family thinking as you do?" He shrank two inches before she finished with him. She took his "That's the way it is and that's the way it always will be" attitude and shoved it down his throat. Hell, I even felt sorry for the poor bastard, and it made me seriously consider turning around and walking the other way. But my curiosity had been aroused, and there was no turning back. This moment reminded me of a time when I was at a family barbecue and my father warned me not to touch the grill because it was hot. Contrary to better judgment and fascinated by the glowing grill, not only did I touch, but I placed both of my hands on it, causing my skin to blister like bubble wrap. She, like the barbecue grill, was red hot, and my need for firsthand knowledge superseded prior warning, so I approached her.

My insides hummed in a frenzy as I came closer to the slender figure outlined in shadow. Instinctually, she spun around to face me. Her face was exquisite, as if uniquely and beautifully painted into place. I froze and could feel a cold sweat begin to build as my brain impulses fired commands to my nerves and muscles. Pressed to act, I began to clap, and said, "Well done, well done." A smirk replaced her perplexed look as she thanked me and turned back toward the bar.

"Do you mind if I sit here?" I asked, touching the torn, brown vinyl barstool next to hers. She nodded in a manner that let me know she couldn't have cared less if I went and sat in a corner with my thumb in my mouth, but I wasn't giving up that easily.

"I'm Vince," I introduced myself and held out my hand.

She tilted her head slightly towards me, pushing a few strands of her wild hair out of her face. Her hair was a crowning touch of long, healthy strands that fell softly into her face, as if knowing how lovely she was and wanting to be nearer. "Nice to meet you, Vince. I'm Skylar."

I smiled nervously as the touching of our hands sent me skyward. Searching for something interesting to say I blurted out, "So, where are you from?" The mundane question echoed fifteen times in my head and her facial expression twitched, as if an internal alarm had gone off, alerting her to a potentially boring conversation. I couldn't believe I had just said that. We sat as the noise level of the crowd increased as she contemplated whether to answer my question or just ignore it and hope that I would slink away.

Deciding to let me stick around she answered, "I'm from Washingtonville; it's about forty-five minutes outside New York City." "How about you?"

"Concord, roughly thirty-five minutes outside San Francisco, traveling east."

"From the West," Skylar said, smiling. "So what brings you out this way, cowboy?" she asked sarcastically. I took a long deep drink of my beer hoping to conjure up some grand story that would not only make me look good, but possibly get me back to her place later that night. But, just as the granddaddy of all lies was about to spill forth from the recesses of my imagination, she interrupted. "Let me guess. You're a recent college grad looking for some real-life experiences since your bubble of comfort had burst." She brought her stool closer, leaned toward me, stared directly into my eyes, and started again. "Maybe you're frustrated. Yeah, plans for graduate school or your dream job didn't quite go as you'd hoped, and now you're here. Why? Because it's better than dealing with your parents and their seemingly endless stream of phone calls that begin with " just calling to say hello," but always end with "So what are you going to do now?" She sat back confidently and stared at me to see if my reaction would reveal if she was close. I just gently moved my stool back and acted like I was looking for something on the floor. "Did you drop something?" she asked.

"Yeah, my jaw dropped somewhere around here. Do you see it?" Pleased with my response she started to smile and then broke into a chuckle.

This moment of levity was exactly what I needed at this moment because the pressure to impress her through embellished tales of my greatness seemed to dissipate as quickly as the distance between us did. I ordered two beers for us and sat back on my stool as the cigarette smoke and smell of booze mingled intoxicatingly with her perfume.

"So why are *you* here?" I asked in an attempt to pull myself together.

"Pretty much the same reasons as you. I just graduated from college and had the urge and opportunity to seek some real-life experiences," she said nonchalantly as she raised the freshly poured beer to her lips for her first sip.

"Where did you go to school?" I queried.

"The College of William and Mary have you ever visited?"

"I haven't but I know it is in colonial Williamsburg where the whole town dresses in eighteenth-century garb and recreates the daily activities from that era, right?"

"Yep. All that kind of got on my nerves. Its quaintness and constant reliving of the past was nice for Williamsburg's tourist draw, but it seemed to overshadow the fact that a fully functioning, twentieth-century institution of higher learning also existed," she explained defensively. "Do you know that three former U.S. presidents attended, including Thomas Jefferson?"

"Hmm, I knew Jon Stewart went there, but I thought Jefferson went to Harvard," I replied hoping to get another chuckle.

"Smart ass" she said glaring at me. "Being the second oldest University in The United States, William and Mary has been educating future leaders almost as long as Harvard," she proudly declared.

"Where were you educated?" she asked changing the subject as if relishing the chance to rip into to my college choice.

" Cal Berkeley" I responded, "Go Bears!" .

"Ah, the Mecca of free speech and free love. So did they turn you into another Mario Savio or a Ted Kaczynski?" Skylar inquired.

"You know it is possible for a person to attend Cal and just be a student not a stereotype."

"Touché," she shot back.

"I'm serious," I said, swallowing the last of my beer. "Look, enough of this college bullshit. Let's discuss what brought us so far from home. Sound good?"

"This really sounds as if you have something interesting to say," drawing her stool closer.

I assured her, "it's more stimulating than which colleges we attended."

"You first," she insisted finishing her beer and ordering two more for us.

"Well, you pretty much guessed how I ended up here. It was

the combination of wanting to do something different and having the plans for my immediate future derailed, except it was
the other way around. See, I wanted to go to law school, but not
just any law school; I'd wanted to go to Harvard ever since I
could remember. When it came time to apply, I only applied to
Harvard, and I got rejected. I guess I thought that since I had always assumed I'd go there, it was fate that I would. Looking back
now, that seems foolish." Her chest rose like she wanted to say
something, but I interrupted. "I know what you're going to
say—I was dumb, arrogant, and unrealistic—I have heard it all
from my friends and family."

Skylar set her beer on the bar and leaned toward me to make
sure the noise level in the bar would not interfere with what she
was about to say. "I don't think you're foolish at all. Personally,
I think it takes guts to do what you did."

"Get rejected?" I asked a little confused.

"No," she stated firmly. "The way I see it, you had a goal.
You wanted to go to law school. However, unlike most people
you knew, there was only one school you wanted to attend. So
rather than writing a dozen applications and personal state-
ments—all emphatically stating how much you want to attend
their school—you had confidence in yourself and your decision
to send only one. Sure, you're more likely to hit a target with a
shotgun spray than with a single shot, but what kind of skill
does that take? You've got the heart of a marksman. I believe
Harvard missed a good lawyer by not accepting you."

I was speechless for a moment after her statement. "I don't
believe it," shaking my head, "The people I have known my
whole life, my family and friends, tell me what an idiot I was,
while you, someone I have known for forty-five minutes, is impressed. I can't believe I had to come all the way to Croatia just
to find someone who could make me feel good about the
decision I made."

"You're welcome, I think," she responded.

"Your turn," I declared.

"Okay, let's see....Well, I'm here because, unlike you, everything worked out for me. I graduated number one in my class, was awarded a Marshall Scholarship, and was accepted at Cambridge University for graduate work. My coming to Croatia came about by accident."

"Accident?" I repeated.

"Yeah," she confirmed. "This gets kind of convoluted, so bear with me. Jane Goodall was scheduled to speak at William and Mary this past year. Having been an admirer of Jane and the work she did, I decided to set up a Jane Goodall information booth. On the day of her lecture, she stopped by the booth and thanked me for doing it. While we spoke, she told me about a new project she was starting called 'Roots and Shoots.' It was targeted at building youth awareness of issues like the environment. To make a long story short, we talked briefly, I told her to keep up the good work, and we went our separate ways. Well, about a week later, after coming home from track practice, I saw a penciled message on the counter informing me that Jane Goodall had called and telling me to give her a return call. At first I thought my roommates were playing a joke on me. Willing to play along, I called the number written on the note, and it rang until a polite voice answered 'Hello?' in an English accent." Skylar put her hand to her ear as if she were on the phone.

"'Dr. Jane?' I asked. 'Why, yes, who's calling?' I started to tremble with excitement as she explained the reason for her call. It had to do with her new project, and she said she would like for me to come to Africa and spend the summer working on the development of the Tanzania Roots and Shoots Club. I told her I would have to get back to her, even though I had already decided to go. She then invites me to lunch and says I can give her an answer then. Two days later, we meet for lunch and I tell her the good news that I would love to go to Africa. Jane was delighted and we tentatively began planning the dates."

I gave her another puzzled look. "Wow, that is fascinating, but how did you get *here*?"

"Oh, right," she said. "I'm sorry. I'm so excited to work with Dr. Jane that I immediately told you that story." I came to Croatia because it seemed like the thing to do. I had the time and had wanted to visit this city for years and I wasn't going to let a war stop me and here I am!"

"This must be fate," I thought to myself as I gazed at her.

Skylar looked at her watch. "Well, it's getting late and I feel these beers sneaking up on me."

"I'm pretty tired myself," I said, lying through my teeth. I could have talked to her all night.

"It was a pleasure meeting you, Vince."

"Likewise," I said. "Hey, what are you doing tomorrow?" I continued. "The reason I ask is because I'm planning to tour the city. Do you want to join me?"

"I'm sorry; I already have plans," she responded. "Maybe we can catch up later on?"

"I hope so," I said, smiling. "I'm staying at the Hotel Panorama."

"Good to know," she responded.

She got up and headed for the door, I followed behind, then quickly got in front of her to open the door and wish her good night. "Good night," she said and walked out. Closing the door I watched her through the glass. Her lean, long limbs flowed so naturally, it was a pleasure to see her move. Look back, look back, look back, I repeated. Then, right before she was out of my sight, she glanced back and smiled.

"Yes!" I whispered to myself as she disappeared into the night.

• • •

I woke up early the next morning and was anxious to explore

Zagreb. I made my way through the cobblestone streets as people interacted in street cafés, retail stores, and places of worship. While walking, I noticed rose bushes with robust blooms of deep red, providing a brilliant contrast to the earth-stained walls of an old house I passed. The sky was clear, and a distant sun cast its warming rays in varying lengths. It was hard to believe that the death and destruction of war was still raging less than 200 miles away in cities much like this one, while here things appeared peaceful. Many of the shell-damaged buildings had been repaired, and while these quick fixes may have helped to hide the effects of war for structures of stone, and wood, I would soon learn the emotional damage upon the people who had escaped the war was much tougher to remedy, especially for the children I interviewed. Throughout the day, I interacted with different youth, letting them know I was a reporter for a newspaper and I wanted to share their stories with my readers back in California. I explained that by putting a human face to their suffering, it might help to draw attention that would grow into to an effort to end the war. Only a few wanted to share their stories. I believe they feared repercussions against their parents if they spoke to the press. However the few children who did share their experiences allowed me to create an op-ed piece that ran in the *San Francisco Chronicle*. One youth I spoke with was twelve-year-old Kenan. He told me his home in Bosnia had been destroyed, and over the past nine months, he, his mother, and his younger brother had lived in a refugee camp outside Zagreb. Kenan's father was not with the family because he was a solider and was fighting in Bosnia. The family had managed to stay in touch with him through letters and believed he was doing well.

"But that was weeks ago," Kenan said, staring at the ground, holding his New York Yankees hat tightly as tears welled up in the corners of his eyes. I asked if he was a Yankees fan.

"Yes!" he replied enthusiastically.

"Would you like to travel to New York someday to see them

play?" I asked, attempting to brighten the mood.

"Yes," he replied, then added, "but only if I can go with my dad."

I had to hear these stories only once to understand the painful truth. The unfortunate casualties of this conflict (or any conflict, for that matter) were the children. At a time in their lives when they needed love and nurturing, they were being exposed to death and destruction.

That evening, I sat up in my spartan room at the Hotel Panorama and wrote. I sustained myself by drinking strong Croatian coffee and eating stale rolls I had smuggled up to my room from breakfast. My words flowed as I was saddened and outraged by what I had seen and heard. Halfway around the world my stories would appear in the *Contra Costa Sun* and would later be picked up by a larger daily paper, the *Contra Costa Times*. The children's emotions fueled my pen as I wrote their stories until the early-morning hours. Finished, I sent the article to my editor via e-mail and finally closed my eyes to get some much needed rest.

• • •

It was barely five in the morning when a loud buzz sounded. Suddenly, thinking it was the fire alarm, I jumped out of bed and stumbled around. The buzz continued, and I finally realized that it was the phone. *"Hello?"* I said in a scratchy, barely audible voice.

"Hello? Vince, is that you ?"

For a moment I was silent trying to think who this was. "Skylar?" I asked with surprise.

"Look, I'm sorry for waking you, but I'm leaving Croatia in an hour, and before I left, I wanted to share some great news," she said, barely able to catch her breath. A strange background echo pulsated through the phone.

"You just got here. Where are you?" I asked.

"Train station. I'm going to Austria, but that is not important. What is important is that you tell me what your plans are for the summer."

"My summer?" I asked.

"Yes! Remember I told you I was going to work with Dr. Jane?"

"Yeah," I replied, not sure of where she was going with this.

"To make a long story short, I spoke with Dr. Jane this past week and we discussed how much work I had to do this summer and she suggested it might be more than one person could do. So yesterday I thought about what she said and then thought about you and then I did it!"

"You did what?" I asked, barely able to contain my curiosity.

" I asked if you could come with me. I told her all about you, recent college grad, seasoned journalist with a passion for all things African—all right, I embellished a bit, but you can fake it. What do you say? Do you want to come to Africa with me?"

As she said those words, I could feel the adrenaline rushing through my veins, my tiredness had vanished and I was filled with excitement.

"Is this a joke?" I asked.

"Of course not! Listen, I know we met just the other night and this seems extremely strange, but bottom line, it is a once-in-a-lifetime chance. Take it!"

There was so much traveling through my head, I just grabbed the first words and blurted them out: "Okay! Okay, I'll go."

"But she's going to Austria," I thought to myself. "When will I see her again? When are we leaving for Africa? I should tell her I changed my mind. This is absurd."

But Skylar had it all worked out. It was as if she'd heard my thoughts, and she proceeded to give me the rundown. "I'll be in Austria for one week," she said. "Then I travel to Bournemouth to meet with Jane and do some preliminary work for Roots and Shoots. Meet me in London. From there we'll fly to Nairobi, and worry about working our way toward Tanzania when we get there. So I'll see you in London a week from tomorrow?" she asked. "I'll be there!" I confirmed.

Slowly hanging up the phone, I looked out my window at the freshly emerging daylight. "Holly Shit!" I said out loud realizing what I had just committed to...I'm going to Africa!

Chapter Two

A week later, Skylar and I arrived at Jomo Kenyatta International Airport. It was close to midnight as we exited the plane and waded through crowds of passengers. Like lemmings, we all huddled close and followed an unknown leader to the customs gate. Having just gotten over a bout of twenty-four-hour flu, I was feeling less than par and hoped that our passage through customs wouldn't take long. This seemed a good possibility since everyone spoke English, which was in fact one of Kenya's official languages. I pulled my oversized suitcase as shrill squeaks erupted from one of the bag's sticking wheels, causing it to roll constantly to the left. Having to make frequent adjustments, I thought to myself, "Why did I bring so much stuff?" However, my load was definitely light in comparison with those who surrounded me. Many people had four or five pieces of luggage. Large cardboard boxes with handles fashioned from tape seemed to be the preferred method of transporting their belongings. I could see the strain in people's faces as they inched themselves closer to the customs window, laboriously dragging their possessions behind them.

"You certainly are traveling light," I said to an elderly gentleman whose only luggage was a small wicker basket with handles. He was silent. I repeated myself a little louder. After a few seconds, the man realized that I was speaking to him, and he turned to face me.

"I'm sorry, young man, what was that you said? You will

have to forgive me, for my hearing isn't what it used to be."

"Oh, it was nothing, really, I was just curious as to why most of the people around us look as if they have brought everything they own, while you manage with just a small basket. I was just thinking aloud and made a stupid observation. Sorry for disturbing you, sir," I said, realizing how intrusive my question must have sounded to a complete stranger. I then noticed that Skylar was waving me over to a customs desk, so I turned to go. Suddenly the elderly man nudged me on the shoulder and said, "Is this your first time in Africa?"

"It sure is," I replied.

"Well then, let me be the first to welcome you to my country," he said, extending his hand.

"Thanks, thanks very much," I responded, adding, "Look, I'm really sorry for asking about your bag. I mean..." I found myself grasping for words, but before I could get an intelligible sentence out, he interrupted.

"You must always remember, no observation, no matter how minute, is ever stupid. In fact, many men I've known have been well served by a keen awareness and observations drawn from their surroundings. You possess a gift that will serve you well not only in Africa, but in life. Don't ever apologize for that." Reflecting on his words, I shook his hand and thanked him again for welcoming us and then hurried to the customs desk to meet Skylar.

Seemingly angry that I had caused him to wait for me, the customs agent motioned Skylar to pass as he ripped the passport from my hands. He asked me a few questions; I replied; he stamped my passport and I smiled as he pushed it into my hand. He then motioned me forward. Skylar anxiously waited for me on the other side of the gate. We had to hurry in order to get a room at a lodge she had just phoned.

Out on the streets, Nairobi was alive. Taxis moved swiftly, darting in and out of traffic. We waited at the taxi ranks for a driver. One came quickly and escorted us from the curb into the backseat of his cab, then put our bags in the trunk. The driver was a pleasant break from the Gestapo-like customs agents. He was exceedingly polite and made us feel comfortable.

"Welcome to Nairobi, my friends. Where will you be heading this evening?" he asked, as if he had rehearsed the line all day. Skylar quickly thumbed through a guidebook as I held the flashlight. While she looked up the lodge, I asked if it was always that busy at the airport. "Oh yes," he answered. "We are the largest city between Cairo and Johannesburg, and growing. We are also one of the most industrialized cities in East Africa, and this attracts businessmen from all over the world, don't ya know?"

"New Kenya Lodge on River Road," Skylar interrupted with satisfaction in her voice because she had finally found the address. She leaned over the front seat and showed it to him.

"Ah yes, the New Kenya Lodge. It is quite a popular place for young travelers, but it is located in a bad part of the city." Skylar and I looked at each other.

"How bad?" I asked.

"I don't want to scare you," he said looking at me through the rearview mirror, "but a lot of trouble brews in that area."

I pushed the topic. "What kind of trouble?"

"Fights, stabbings, robbery, an occasional shooting, you know, trouble," he cautioned us, emphasizing the word *trouble*. "Just stay away from the bars and you will be fine. Only the troublemakers are out at this time of night. Just stay away from the bars," he repeated. That sounded easy enough.

As the taxi rolled on, I sat back and watched the city slowly transform from bustling, well-lit streets with well-dressed people in evening clothes strolling on the sidewalks to dark, empty streets and menacing alleys with vagrants searching for remnants of food in garbage cans. The inhabitants in this section mostly were on midnight stumbles instead of strolls, while others huddled in secrecy, no doubt consummating some illegal deal according to our taxi driver. It was sad to see that not much changes about city life, no matter what part of the world one is in. Poverty has no boundaries; it infects and corrupts whatever it touches like a persistent viral infection. This was the forgotten part of Nairobi that is rarely seen, hidden from view like an unwanted child. In fact, the driver told us that had we been business clients or prospective investors in Nairobi, he might have been instructed by the local businesspeople not to drive through this area at night. Gone from sight were the Ambassador and Hilton hotels and the expensive eating and shopping establishments that were on the other side of Tom Mboya Street, the road that divided the city into two parts based on economics and class structure.

We turned onto River Road, and as I looked around, I realized that staying away from bars was going to be more difficult than anticipated, for everything on the street seemed to be either a pub, a pub/restaurant, or a disco. The street unfolded like a carnival, with all types of people walking about. This particular section was lit up from signs and lights that ran the length of most buildings. "Here we are," announced the driver as he put the car in park and turned off the engine. The building was narrow but tall and didn't look nearly as bad as I had imagined. I thanked the driver, and when I tipped him, he smiled and told me one last time, "Check in and stay in. Look around tomorrow. Only the devious are out at this late hour over here." I wondered, if he had been a decade younger, would he have given us the same advice? To be honest, it really didn't look that bad. Sure, it was loud and dirty and smelled as if an open sewer line was nearby, but I sometimes got that same impression while walking the city streets back home. There was a gated entrance with a doorbell that presumably sounded in the manager's office. Skylar rang the bell, and an annoying buzzing sound signaled that we could let ourselves in. Directly ahead of us was a long, narrow flight of stairs. Skylar sighed in exhaustion. I grabbed her bag and said, "Here, let me."

She gave me a look of thanks and then hugged and sponta-
neously kissed me before climbing the stairs to go check us in!
There it was, our first kiss! It felt good and in fact it carried with
it a sense of intrigue and adventure.

Inspired by this unexpected kiss, I continued to slowly make
my way up the steep, narrow staircase, which resembled a gang-
way on a ship. The bags were bulky and heavy, and with them,
I barely fit into the narrow passage. Squeezing through I heard
a crunching sound that came from an outside pocket of one of
the bags. Reaching in I noticed a stack of plastic cups, forks,
moist towelettes, and a few other items Skylar had packed for
our convenience. "She thought of everything," I thought impressed. A couple came in behind me and tried to rush past.
Frustrated, I climbed as quickly as I could, which caused me to
smash my pinkie between the metal handle of Skylar's bag and
the rail. Clenching my teeth in pain, I moved to put the injured
pinkie in my mouth, but then realized this was impossible to do
without dropping the bag on top of the couple behind me, which
didn't sound like such a bad idea at this point. Realizing what
had happened, the couple asked if they could help me. "No
thanks, I've got it, just give me a minute," I said, looking sternly
at the guy as I thought, "Why didn't you offer as soon as you
saw me struggling?" I continued my ascent and they began
speaking German. I assumed that they were talking about me.
When I finally reached the top of the stairs, I released the bags
from my aching hands. A deep crease ran across each hand
where a handle had dug into the flesh, cutting off blood circula-
tion. My pinkie was throbbing. The couple rushed around me
and I shouted, "Nice meeting you!"

Across the room, Skylar was smiling as if she were having a
pleasant chat with the manager, who turned out to be the owner
as well. He introduced himself as Ken and was from Australia,
but quickly said "the only thing that remains truly Australian

about me is my accent. I'm fifty-one years old and I've spent thirty-one of those years here in Kenya. Yes, I believe I'm more African than Australian," he proudly declared then went on to check us in. "Now, your room is located in the open lodging area. I'm sorry, but that's all I have at this late hour."

His apology told me that this "open lodging" probably wasn't that great, but I was tired and told him, "Hey, as long as you have clean sheets on the bed, I don't care where you put us." Skylar concurred.

"That's the spirit," he said, handing us a padlock and a key. "As you will soon notice, there are no locks on the doors. That is what this is for. Lock it when you sleep and whenever you leave the room. Understand?"

"Yes, sir," Skylar responded sternly. He wished us a good night; we offered the same and left for our room.

• • •

The room more closely resembled an office cubicle than a hotel room. It was small, roughly six feet by eight feet, with two small beds with baby-blue sheets and white pillows. A lone wooden chair stood in the corner. The walls of the room were disjointed from the ceiling and the floor. There was a four-foot gap between the ceiling and the top of the walls and about an eighteen-inch gap between where the walls ended and the floor began. Needless to say, we could hear exactly what everybody else was doing on this floor. Privacy was not an option, which was probably why the owner had apologized for having to put us here. Since we were a couple, he naturally assumed that we would want to be alone on our first night in Africa, and he knew that was impossible in this room. Snoring, belching, and other bodily functions erupted all around us. One guy was even yelling in his sleep. We couldn't make out what he was saying, but boy, could he yell. Skylar and I began to snicker.

"Welcome to Africa," I announced, as I jumped on top of one of the beds with my arms wide open. Our laughter mounted until we were at the point where we could no longer talk and our stomachs ached.

Then somebody shouted in broken English, "Shut the hell up over there!" This gave us a first-class case of the giggles that we couldn't stop. We tried to keep it down and laugh under our breath, but the giggles escaped and we continued to laugh aloud. As the "quiets" and "shut ups" increased, we realized that we had awakened nearly half the people on the floor.

"I'm gonna take a shower before these people lynch us," I said, still in hysterics.

"Me too," Skylar giggled back. I went to the men's showers upstairs, and she headed for the women's facilities just down the hall. As I walked upstairs, I could still hear her giggling in the distance.

I stood in the doorway of the shower room. There was a light hanging from the ceiling. The bulb was attached to a ceramic fixture, and amazingly, it turned on when I pulled on the dangling metal chain. What a depressing sight, I thought to myself. The floor was a pathetic collage of exposed concrete and cracked black and white ceramic tile. Some of the windows were missing, and the ones that remained were filthy; you probably couldn't see through them even during daylight. Metal security screens covered each window, but the locks had rusted away and now hung useless as the gray paint buckled from weathering and neglect. The once-white enamel sink basin was now chipped and brownish streaks ran from the rust while the copper faucets were covered in patina and leaky. The mirror above the sink was cracked and the silvering showed through in some places. And the toilets stank with the smell of stale urine and looked like they had never been cleaned. Strange insects, possibly flies but unlike any flies I had seen, buzzed around me as I swatted to keep them from landing on me after they had just come from the toilet.

A large, square doorway led to the shower. A thin layer of green slime rose from the exposed concrete floor as tiny organisms grew into thriving populations, and small patches of mold resembling the shapes of continents grew on the walls. From one of these walls sprouted a rusty pipe with tiny droplets of water suspended at the end. This was my shower—or water pipe, to be more precise, for what I saw did not resemble any shower I had seen before. Hanging from the pipe was a sign that read: Hot Water Only in the Evening. There was nothing more that I could have asked for at that moment than a hot shower. I stripped down and hung my clothes on a broken brass wall hanger. I stepped into the shower and felt the tiny organisms beneath my feet. As I applied more weight to my step, I almost slipped. I turned the handle and out shot a stream of water. I let it heat up for a few seconds, then stepped in front of it. The water was a perfect temperature and had a slight aroma of kerosene. The hot water and soap felt great. I worked up a thick soap lather removing the layer of sweat and dirt that had accumulated during the many hours of travel. I was finally in Africa.

As I entered the room, Skylar sat on her bed, combing through her long, wild, dirty-blonde hair. The smell of fresh flowers permeated the air. "How was your shower?" she asked with a smile.

"Refreshing," I replied. "How about yours?" I asked, draping my clothes over the back of a wooden chair.

"Wonderful," she exclaimed. "It feels so good to be clean." I nodded in agreement. We folded back the stiff, freshly washed sheets and eased our clean bodies into bed. When I was finally comfortable, I sighed, turned off the light, and said good night to Skylar. By now it was 2:30 a.m., and as I lay on my back trying to drift to sleep, my mind became absorbed by the crazy thought of what would happen if someone tried to climb over the wall and into our room. I opened my eyes and stared at the darkness, imagining a pair of eyes peering at me to make sure I was asleep. Then a head emerged, an arm, followed by a leg. Then the rest of a body slowly came over the wall. He hung there for a second, then dropped silently into my room.

"Jesus," I thought as a chill came over me. The driver's words echoed in my ears: "A lot of trouble brews in that area, fights, stabbings, robberies, an occasional shooting..." I had to devise a system that would alert me if someone entered the room. Skylar was sound asleep but I was searching the recesses of my mind for something that might alert us, and then remembered the stack of plastic cups. I got up and quietly dug through Skylar's bag. "Aha!" I declared as I felt the plastic cups against my hand. With my small flashlight, I carefully placed a dozen or so of them strategically around the room so that, with the lights out, there would be no way of successfully negotiating through them. I was a light sleeper, and the sound of the crushing cups would definitely wake me. Sitting at the foot of my bed, I looked proudly at my improvised security scheme. I knew it wasn't foolproof, but it was better than nothing, and if anything, it restored my peace of mind enough so I could finally close my eyes.

• • •

A loud cracking sound awakened me. "Oh no, someone has climbed over the wall," I thought. Paralyzed by fear and disbelief, I hesitated, but finally threw back the sheets, jumped up and steadied my fists trying to focus in on the intruder.

"Ouch, what the hell was that?" a voice uttered. "Oops", I thought to myself, it was Skylar who had gotten up for some reason. "What are all these cups doing on the floor?" she queried as she stood there in confusion.

"I set the cups around the room to warn us in case anyone tried to climb over the wall to rob or, worse, kill us." It worked!" I exclaimed picking up the crushed cup.

She looked up at the wall, then down to the floor, and finally at me asking. "How long did you stay up to figure this little scheme out?"

"About an hour," I responded, trying to figure out whether she thought me a raving loony.

"Good thinking, but maybe a little paranoid?" she questioned with a smile.

"Honestly, if I had been alone, I would not have done it, but I have you to think about and I didn't want to take even the slightest chance," I said earnestly, remembering the kiss she had given me earlier. She looked shocked by my statement (being the independent, no-nonsense, I-can-take-care-of-myself kind of woman that she was). But her cheeks turned rosy, making it impossible for her to hide that she was flattered, maybe even honored, that I thought her to be a treasure worthy of guarding.

Chapter Three

The next morning, the sun was bright and the temperature seemed to rise with each passing minute. We left our room with a click of the padlock. Making our way down stairs and out into the morning, we shaded our eyes initially as they adjusted to the daylight. I noticed River Road had been transformed from a haven for drunks and mischievous merchants to a populous market and trading center where the entire city converged. The area was full of color. Red, green, purple, brown, yellow, and orange all mixed in harmony as fruit stalls stood next to handmade basket stalls. Leather stalls stood next to flower stalls. The area's visual confusion was responsible for its beauty. Some vendors stood in front of their stalls attracting customers, while others haggled prices from behind a display. It was an incredible scene. I realized that the driver had given me an incomplete impression of this area. It was true that this was where the unemployed, disenfranchised, and wily operated. However, this was also where the little guy tried to make a buck by providing services and goods that could be found for a cheaper price here than in other parts of the city. This attracted the middle class from the suburbs, as well as the wealthy and powerful. River Road had the type of flair one might compare to Telegraph Avenue in Berkeley. It, too, was a place where tourists, doctors, lawyers, and students coalesced with store-owners, food vendors, prostitutes, the destitute, and manual laborers.

It was still early, and Skylar suggested we find a restaurant to have some breakfast. "You read my mind," I said, salivating at the thought of food. We ducked into a little breakfast spot that was light and cheery inside. The tables and chairs were white and pink and belonged in an ice cream parlor. The pictures on the wall were of warm, tropical vacation places like Hawaii, St. Tropez, and Tahiti and belonged in a travel agency. However, the heterogeneous touches made it warm and welcoming. I found it to be a refreshing change from the uniformity found in many eating establishments in the United States. In fact, the restaurant reminded me of the types of eating places my grandparents had frequented many years earlier in the sprawling farm town of Santa Rosa, California.

The bell behind the door had rung, alerting the staff to our presence. The place seemed popular with few seats available, but I did spot a table by the window and indicated we would like to be seated there. "As you wish," said a slender Indian server holding menus and utensils wrapped in napkins. We examined the menu, ordered a pot of tea, "eggs, omelet style" as the menu read, and toast.

Skylar sat next to me so that she, too, could look out the window to see the activities in the street. We stared outside and into the lives of those on the street. One shoeless man in particular caught my eye as he approached another man and asked for a cigarette. The man shoved him aside and passed. He sat back down, and then stood up again to ask the next passerby for a smoke. This second man was not necessarily down and out, but I could tell by his demeanor that he was no stranger to the shoeless man's situation. He handed him a cigarette. Then the shoeless man searched his pockets desperately for a light, but gave up and looked at the second man as if to say, "That's how bad things have gotten." The man quickly reached into his pocket to retrieve a pack of matches, lit the shoeless man's cigarette, then his own. As he went to put the matches back in his pocket, he hesitated and then handed them to the shoeless man, along with an extra smoke. The shoeless man thanked him, reaching out and clasping his hands. The shoeless man, now content, sat down to smoke his cigarette. He now had a pack of matches and a cigarette, and he seemed to take solace in knowing he was better off now than he had been two minutes earlier.

The man looked around: first left, then right, then left again. He looked down at the ground or maybe at his shoeless feet. His trousers were badly soiled and his hair was matted. Small pieces of lint and debris were nestled in it. He was shirtless, perhaps toothless, and his skin was as black as pitch. I pried myself away and turned to our food, which had just arrived. I looked at Skylar and could tell the scene out the window had not escaped her either.

We both ate with reduced appetites, but agreed that the eggs tasted better here than at home. Suddenly, Skylar uttered, "In general, life is harsh on a person, but I often wonder where people like him find the strength to go on when life becomes unbearable." I didn't answer her because I didn't know. Turning our attention once again to the outside scene, the man was now laughing. Two other men, who appeared to share similar lots in life, joined him. All three sat sharing the cigarette, talking and smiling in the sunlight. At the moment, life was good for them.

• • •

By noon, we had explored the entire area immediately surrounding our lodge and were now back at the New Kenya, informing Ken we had decided to stay another night. Delighted, he fixed us up with a larger, more private room. "You mean a room with full walls, a ceiling, and insulation from other guests' disgusting bodily functions and sleeping disorders?" I sarcastically exclaimed.

"Oh come now, it wasn't that bad, and if you keep that tone, I'll give your girl the new room and you'll spend another night in 225," he volleyed back.

Laughing, I went to collect our bags from the first room and put them in the iron storage cage located down a long hall near the back of the hotel. The attendant told me our bags would be safe here while our new room was being tidied. When I returned to the front desk, Ken was speaking to Skylar, asking if we had been exploring all morning. Skylar responded, "Yes we have, but just the wrong side of Tom Mboya Street," smiling mischievously.

"Well then, my dear, you and your mate should definitely head across the road to see how the other half lives on the proper side of Tom Mboya." Ken insisted there was a fine selection of restaurants and pubs that, for the quality, were "quite reasonably priced." Having spent just over four dollars for our room and breakfast, I was quite happy with the accommodation and food on this part of Tom Mboya Street. But Skylar was eager to explore more and take a tour of Nairobi National Park so we were off.

We walked a good mile before seeing an available taxi. We were lucky, for usually taxis cannot be hailed from the streets. Instead of searching for customers, they wait at taxi ranks located where the need is most likely to be concentrated, such as near the railroad station or the best hotels. As we made our way across Tom Mboya Street and into the "proper" side, the buildings gradually grew taller, the landscaping improved, and the streets were cleaner. The smell of burning tires, which filled the air on the bad side, seemed to dissipate as we continued toward the more cosmopolitan part of Nairobi.

Inside the cab, I had my window down to provide some comfort from the overpowering smell of our driver's perspiration. I wasn't a jerk about it; in fact I kept it to myself, because I knew this guy was working hard, and his beat up Datsun 510 didn't afford him the luxury of air-conditioning. It was like an oven inside the cab. The black leatherette interior absorbed the heat like a sponge, and I'd burned the hell out of the back of my legs when I first jumped in the front seat. The driver had a small wicker seat cover that provided a thin layer of insulation between him and the seat, in order to reduce perspiration from long hours of driving. He glanced out his window as one of the brand-new London taxis passed him with all the windows up. He knew the driver of that cab wasn't drowning in his sweat. I sensed his envy as he commented on the excessive speed of the driver in the new cab. "They always show off like that, but without his fancy car, he is no better than me, no better," he said, now concentrating on the road ahead of him .

Not knowing exactly where to go, we asked the driver where he thought the best location to drop us might be. He suggested the Hilton; whether he really thought this was the best place to drop us was debatable because he seemed so preoccupied, but we agreed and he made a quick left to adjust our direction.

The energy level seemed to dwindle compared with the area where we were staying. We rolled down hotel- and office-lined streets as people in suits hurried about on a busy work day. This may have been the proper side of Tom Mboya Street, but it sure seemed a lot duller.

The tourist population also seemed to lose its flair and image of adventure. Rather than seeing youthful trekkers with shabby backpacks, well-worn hiking boots, and unshaven faces and legs, one now observed elderly, overweight men and women wearing obnoxious pastel clothing and sporting big hats. They gathered in clusters mostly in front of the nicer hotels and museums. In a serious voice I asked Skylar, "What new species of African wildlife do you reckon those are?" as I pointed to a cluster of them.

Skylar, who was a good sport, rolled with it. "Well now, let me take a look at this safari guidebook I have. Let's see now, hmm, how strange, I cannot seem to find a picture that looks quite like that," pointing to a group of them sitting on a bench and fanning themselves. By this time the driver had caught on to what we were doing and surprisingly got a good laugh. It was nice to see him express such approval and enjoyment of our sardonic banter. He had initially appeared beyond laughter in his pensive state but had proved us wrong.

The cab slowed. "The Hilton," he said, pointing to a large multistory building of glass, steel, and concrete located across the street

"Excellent," I replied.

"That will be sixty shillings, please," he said politely. I handed him sixty-five, and he thanked me and hurried to assist his next fare. I didn't know if tipping was expected or not, but I did it anyway.

Eager to find out how to arrange a tour of the National Park we asked a passing police officer if he could help us. He was very pleasant, and pointed to the place we were already headed, the Hilton. We quickly crossed the street and entered the lobby. We were greeted by a doorman and directed to the front desk. There we proceeded to book a private tour on an air conditioned bus with lunch provided, and all for a very reasonable price. However when we failed to produce a key or the last name of a registered guest they were no longer interested in helping us and said we would have to find a tour leaving from another location. Disappointed, we started to leave. Just then, a bellhop who had overheard our situation approached us and said in a thick, deep voice, "Hello, my name is John and I can help you get a tour of the park". He walked with us outside and pointed to a row of windowed passenger vans. "You can take a nice day trip to the National Park aboard one of those. Come back around two o'-clock and you can purchase a ticket from the driver and be on your way."

We both enthusiastically thanked him for his help and offered him a tip for his time, but he refused and said "it was my pleasure."

It was now just passed 1:00 in the afternoon, and having some time to kill before our departure we decided to grab a bite to eat. Even with the adrenaline coursing through our bodies, in anticipation of our visit our first African game park, we were both hungry. While walking the streets our noses lead us to the pleasant smells coming from a small bakery and decided something from there would suit us just fine. Entering, we were engulfed by the warm aroma of freshly baked breads and pastries. The sparsely furnished establishment had a long metal and glass counter near the center of the back wall filled with baked treasures. On an opposite wall hung a large picture of Daniel arap Moi, president of Kenya. In fact, it was the only thing on the walls except for several layers of fresh white paint. Ladies in white aprons greeted us and stood at attention behind the counter. As Skylar and I examined the goodies, a baker emerged from the back with a sheet of freshly baked brown rolls. He carefully placed the sheet on an open rack to cool, then returned to the back. As steam rose, it carried such a pleasant aroma it was hard to ask for anything else. Just then, the baker emerged once more, this time carrying a sheet of fresh, hot white rolls. "Oh no, those look great too," I said, mesmerized by the golden glow one could almost taste. "We would like three of each, please" One of the women behind the counter carefully retrieved our rolls as if not to disturb their pristine shapes.

With hasty steps we exited the shop, back toward a bench located near where the van would depart. Now seated, I gently broke open two rolls that revealed steamy fluffy centers. I pulled my Swiss Army knife from my pocket and cut a butter pat in half, then placed a half on each roll and squeezed the halves gently back together just for a few seconds. This was just enough time for the heat to melt the butter perfectly. I handed Skylar hers and for the next 20 minutes we alternated "mmms" with each other. The first bites were exquisite, and the second ones even better. We continued until four of the six rolls were gone.

It was then that I noticed my watch now read five minutes until two. Skylar wrapped the remaining rolls and stuffed them into her backpack. I wiped my knife, nearly cut my finger trying to fold it, and then shoved it into my back pocket. Walking toward our van we noticed the driver standing outside enthusiastically greeting passengers as he sold us tickets. We got the last open seat located near the sliding door. I sat first and Skylar slid onto my lap. Looking out the window, I noticed John standing in front of the Hilton waving to us. I nudged Skylar. She looked over, smiled, gave him the thumbs up and with a turn of the key we were off.

The air-conditioning wasn't working, making the air inside the van humid and causing our perspiration to build. I looked up at Skylar as she held her stomach and whispered to me that she felt nauseous from the heat and the occasional waft of body odor. I asked the driver if he could turn on the small fan he had plugged into his cigarette lighter, to which he quickly responded "of course." The fan was surprisingly effective and managed to lower the temperature inside the van just enough to make the 20 minute trip to the park much more pleasant.

Arriving at the park we drove through the gate. The driver pulled over and disappeared into an office under a huge shade tree. Outside the office sat a weary-looking security guard. He had his hat pulled down, nearly covering his eyes as he sat, feet stretched out and arms folded as his AK-47 hung from the back of his chair. His head tipped forward, causing his hat to fall to the ground. Immediately, his arms shot into the air and let out a yawn, then he slowly pulled his arms back to rest on his chest. He squinted as he tried to focus on his surroundings. He wore tan short pants, a matching collared shirt, and a pair of haggard leather boots. As he stood up for a bigger stretch, opening his callused hands and walking a bit, his legs were a display of muscle and sinewy tissue and his calves showed like boulders with every step. He went to a nearby water pump and proceeded to cool off. Even though his shirt was dirty, he carefully took it off and handled it as if it had just come from the cleaners, placing it neatly on a large rock. He put his head under the spigot and proceeded to pump with one arm. This was no simple task, but he managed with ease as his back displayed a similar tangle of sinewy muscle under a dark, glistening layer of skin. He looked more machine than man, and had it not been for his very human expressions, I would have thought him one. Refreshed, he returned to his post outside the office door.

The temperature inside the van had cooled considerably while we waited. The branches from the large tree covering the office reached over like long, sprawling, bushy fingers that provided shade for us as well. The driver returned to the van and stuck his head through the open window on the passenger's side, welcomed us again and shouted, "Wake up, sleepy man" to a guy in the rear of the van. All of us laughed as the poor guy was startled awake. I could tell by his facial expression he was contemplating shouting a few choice words back, but out of better judgment and courtesy, refrained.

The driver introduced himself as Christian. "I will be your guide," he explained with typical tour-guide formality. He continued, "The Nairobi National Park is only a few kilometers from the city center, yet one can see a remarkable selection of African wildlife, if you don't mind an occasional jumbo jet in the background. It is the most accessible of all Kenya's game parks and a perfect place to acquaint oneself with some of the legendary wildlife of the continent."

Christian continued to talk as I tuned out and focused on what lay in front of me. It was a vast area that seemed to broaden and unfold with every mile we drove. I looked out onto brownish green plains spattered with mustard yellow. To my right and near the road we traveled, bones were scattered. I could imagine the process—the unfortunate animal ravaged by a lion or some other predator, leaving only a carcass, which was then scavenged by hyenas and vultures. Finally, insects, such as beetles, would do their job, leaving what I saw before me - scattered bones bleached by the sun's intensity.

The sky was a crisp blue with just a slight accent of fluffy white clouds. They seemed to welcome us as we bounced down the dirt trail. I was topside. The van had a pop-up skylight window that would open so that passengers could stick their heads out, and that became my perch at first. In spite of my initial disappointment, I was determined to make the best of it and see everything I could. We continued to rumble down the roads, all of us soaking in as much as we could. We stopped occasionally, affording an opportunity to get out of the van for a closer look.

One of these areas was near the Mokoyeti Gorge, at the Mbagathi River. Around the river's banks the park was at its most lush, filled with dark green foliage with light green highlights. It provided us an oasis during a day that topped out at 103 degrees Fahrenheit. This was where I spotted a hippopotamus, playing in the river with its dirty brown water, thick muddy shores, and large protruding rocks which actually proved not to be rocks at all, but the backs of other hippopotamuses. "Amazing," I thought. It was the first time I had ever seen animals of this sort in their natural environment and not in some prefabricated replica. It was also the first time I didn't wonder if they were happy in captivity. Except for the regulated intrusion of sightseers like me, their lives were relatively unchanged from that of their parents and grandparents, and they were possibly better off than previous generations since poaching had largely been eliminated in parks like this.

I walked closer to the water's edge, carefully placing my steps so I wouldn't sink ankle-deep in mud. I knelt and resisted movement of any kind. I patiently watched the hippos as they huddled with only the tops of their backs, their ears, eyes, and gaping nostrils above water. The rest of their bodies were submerged, and they resembled dark gray submarines cruising the surface in the murky waters. It was relaxing to watch these mammoth beasts, some as heavy as two tons, gracefully slice through the water. They appeared to be very social mammals because the ones I viewed were in packs ranging from fifteen to thirty.

The hippopotamuses were the biggest mammals I saw that day. Although the others were far smaller, it was still exciting to see animals such as hyenas, vultures, and warthogs in their natural environment. I was disappointed that the more exciting animals like lions, leopards, and cheetahs were nowhere to be seen. Even the usually plentiful supply of zebras, giraffes, and buffalo were sparse and viewed from distances that disappointed. "This is very unusual," Christian explained. "It may be due to the fact that there are other water sources located outside the park. The animals had dispersed and were not necessarily concentrated within the boundaries of the park. "As the months dragged on, however, and the water dried up in these external sources, he continued, the animals would be drawn back into the park and to the plentiful water sources that had been assured through small dams erected on the Mbagathi River."

Further disappointment emerged when "Elephants will not be seen in this park," spilled out of the driver's mouth. "The habitat is not suitable for them to survive here," he said. Sensing the collective aura of disappointment, he quickly added, "But rhinoceroses thrive here, and we may have a good opportunity to see some." The driver further explained that poachers prefer more remote areas to perform their despicable work, but even so, we didn't see one rhinoceros.

• • •

I don't want to give the wrong impression, but the park did not live up to my expectations. It was obvious that the people who operated these grounds cared for them. The park was well maintained. But maintenance wasn't the crux of my frustration. Part of my frustration lay within the images that I had developed of the Nairobi National Park as a child. For it was within this park that Mutual of Omaha's *Wild Kingdom* was filmed. Every Sunday evening around six o'clock, my family and I would gather around the television after dinner, enjoying some dessert creation prepared by my mother, since Sunday night was designated treat night; the lemon frosting drops were my favorite. Marlin Perkins would narrate this wildlife adventure as we all settled into our chairs, anticipating glimpses into the unknown continent of Africa and its greatest treasure: wildlife. I remember images of Perkins and his colleagues making their way across the plains by helicopter, Range Rover, or on foot in pursuit of lions, rhinos, or whatever the particular animal of study was for that week. As I looked around me now, however, all I saw were white Nissan vans with pop tops—all popped—and people walking around pretending to be Marlin Perkins. Most of them were clad in khaki shorts; brand-new, expensive hiking boots; white shirts; and large safari hats in beige, brown, and olive green. Then the bags: They all had bags, many bags, with cameras and camera equipment and multiple lenses, most of which looked like they had never been used before. Most of these people looked as if they had taken up this hobby only hours before they departed for Africa. The harder they tried to look like genuine wildlife photographers, the more they looked like charlatans. Laughing at my own judgmental and somewhat unreasonable expectations, I kept my opinion to myself so as to not tarnish Skylar's experience. Looking across from where I stood, she seemed to be enjoying the tour. At that moment, she caught me glancing at her and she smiled. "Yep, she was enjoying it just fine."

For most of the four-hour tour, we were surrounded by up to twenty white Nissan vans at a time. Then you had to deal with the crowds, the people snapping pictures, and all the other complications that I associated with urban life. This was the reason for much of my frustration. It just wasn't what I was seeking. Additionally, you know what you are getting in urban areas because one expects to be surrounded by people, but here I wanted to be alone, and I had expected to find exotic animals and experience the tranquility of the largest wide-open space I had ever seen.

As I moped, the driver noticed and asked, "Why are you not out looking around, man? Do you not like the outdoors?"

"No, it is quite the opposite," I answered. "I love the outdoors, but have you ever imagined how something was going to be, and even though you never actually experienced it, you were convinced it actually was the way you pictured it? Then when you actually *do* experience it, it's completely different, but in a bad sense of different?"

"You mean you thought the park was going to look like that TV show, *Wild Kingdom*, right?" Smiling, I then went on to enthusiastically share my whole litany of complaints and observations as the driver listened in earnest. Suddenly we were interrupted by a shriek, and being the closest driver, he had to find out what the trouble was. As it turned out, some guy, despite being warned, had attempted to feed one of the little bush monkeys, and it nearly bit off his finger. I didn't care much because he was warned, and I was eager to continue my conversation with the driver.

As we all piled back into the van and embarked upon the last hour of our tour, the driver seemed to break away from the crowd of vans. He was going just fast enough to put some real distance between us and the others. Up ahead was a designated stop area, but before we got there, he indicated that it would be pretty much the same as the last few stops, and if we kept on going, we could create a mile of cushion between us and the rest of the pack and stop in another spot. He had been really listening when I spoke to him. And so for the last leg of the tour,

Christian's talking points were a little more in-depth, his tone a little more nationalist, a little more African. He now seemed proud to be showing us his park near the city in which he was born and raised, and his pride spilled forth like an overfilled glass. He even shared stories about his childhood and youth, his parents and grandparents, and how much the area had changed over the course of many years.

The remaining minutes of the tour clicked away, and we found ourselves arriving back at the gates from which we began. The guard who sat watch had left; only his empty chair remained. A man emerged from the office, waving good-bye as he prepared to close for the day. The sound of voices exploded all around me, and it seemed as if everyone, with the exception of the driver and me, was engaged in conversation. I just sat there and looked out the window. I watched a vulture standing on the edge of a small pool of black water. It made for an excellent mirror, and the vulture seemed to be staring at itself in amazement, as if seeing its reflection for the first time. I wondered if the vulture knew it was staring at itself. Even as we drove closer, his gaze did not waver. The vulture just stood there, fascinated. Shockingly, that image seemed to capture exactly how I was feeling. It was as if I had only just now sat back and wondered: Is this my life? Am I really in Africa, and am I really going to be living and working with Dr. Jane Goodall? The answer? Yes, I was, and Dar es Salaam, where Skylar and I had arranged to meet Dr. Goodall—lay only a few hundred miles southwest of here.

Chapter Four

It was just past six in the evening as we rode back into town dusty and tired. Dinnertime, and Skylar and I were looking forward to a good meal. Skylar had become acquainted with a young British couple on the park tour, and they told her of a great place to have dinner.

We made our way quickly to the corner of Wabera and Kaunda Streets and entered a cozy Italian place called Trattoria, which means "kitchen" in Italian

Having lived three houses down from my Italian grandmother and grandfather, or Nonna and Nonno as we more commonly called them, I had spent a good deal of my life in an authentic Italian-American kitchen, so I had become quite a virtuoso, if you will, on good Italian food. Rosemary and thyme were as common as salt and pepper at my grandmother's table, and this helped to make anyone's dining experience a pleasant one. On a nightly basis, my Nonna would prepare all sorts of recipes that her mother had brought over from Italy. These were dishes that my grandmother had eaten as a kid on her family's 112-acre fruit ranch in Healdsburg, California. The dishes ranged from homemade ravioli and other pastas to tender meats seasoned to perfection with garlic, herbs, and spices. My favorites included gnocchi with pesto, and polenta smothered in a creamy, soft, white Teleme cheese. The gravies my Nonna prepared were made from a combination of a few simple ingredients, Italian sausage, ground sirloin, fresh tomatoes, garlic, and onions. Nobody ever knew the exact measurement for each ingredient added, and to tell you the truth, I don't think she did either. That way, she could keep her recipes a secret. Yes, her dishes were taste-bud tantalizers that would leave my friends talking for weeks about "how good that meal was at your Nonna's house!".

As we entered, the hostess welcomed us and sat us at a table for two nestled in a corner with a perfect view of the city streets. The place was busy, and the aroma's coming from the kitchen promised our meal would be good. Our waiter introduced himself, "Good evening, my name is Samuel and I'm here to serve you." Samuel appeared to be no more than 15 and was clearly a little nervous. "Nice to meet you Samuel," Skylar responded, we are delighted you will be serving us this evening!" "Would you like to start with something to drink?" He asked politely. And then quickly added, "Fresh bread will be coming shortly if you wish," before we could answer his question and then shyly lowered his head as if he thought he had been impolite. "Both sound lovely Samuel!" Skylar responded while also reaching out to place her hand on Samuel's arm as if to assure him he was doing fine. "Please bring us the bread and two glasses of red wine... this Chianti sounds lovely." She indicted pointing at the menu. "Excellent choice Miss" he said smiling as he left the table.

Skylar began to pull her hair back into a ponytail and simultaneously asked "how did you like the tour?" I hesitated, and thought to say something other than the truth but decide against that. "Honestly, I didn't." I said looking down as I placed my napkin on my lap. "I was going to say something but you looked like you were having a great time so hell, I didn't want to ruin your experience just because it didn't live up to my expectations." She leaned into the table and squeezed my left hand "I felt the same way!" she said with a combination look of relief and excitement. "I thought you were having a great time and it was I that would ruin your experience so I kept if to myself!" I was speechless and she started to laugh. All I could think of was how lucky I was to have found such a great travel partner, having barley even known each other when we agreed to this adventure.

I was about to share this with her when Samuel returned to the table with the fresh bread and our wine. "Have you had a chance to look at the menu?" He asked. "Not yet, but do you have any recommendations for us?" I asked. Standing up straight he confidently stated, "My friends *everything* is good!" "Everything?" Skylar responded. "Yes Miss," he replied nodding his head slightly. Samuel then suggested that if we told him which types of dishes we like, pasta, meat, vegetable, or a combination, he would order for us. I was just wondering what happened to the shy boy who only 20 minutes ago was nervous and unsure of himself, but was now confident enough to order for us? "Well I'm game," Skylar said smiling at Samuel. "How about it?" she asked as both of them looked at me. "You only live once, lets go for it!" I said agreeing but not sure I totally agreed. However, in listening to Samuel proceed to make his recommendations with such passion and enthusiasm it no longer mattered if it was good or not. However, as it turned out the food was amazing! We sampled a variety of the specialty items, from the house-cured prosciutto and salami, to the perfectly aged cheeses. Every bite was complimented perfectly with the wine and bread. Next we shared a vegetable infused pasta with a red gravy that admittedly rivaled my Nonna's, and then a meat dish with a combination of flavor so unique that I could honestly say I had never tasted anything like it, nor had Skylar.

Calling Samuel over to inquire about the unique flavor, Samuel shared that "all the recipes originated from my great grandfather who served as part of the kitchen staff for one of the governing Italian officials in Mogadishu when Somalia was still an Italian colony." He went on to tell us his great grandfather learned all the basic techniques and flavor combination from the head chef who originated from the southern part of Italy. Over the years, the recipes were passed down and slowly the original recipes were infused with traditional Somali spices to create what you have tonight. Everything is authentic Italian but with a Somali twist!" He did a twisting motion with his hand. "So everything is to your satisfaction?" "Above and beyond satisfaction Samuel" Skylar announced with her hand across her chest leaning back into her chair. He slightly nodded his head in thanks and left us to continue our meal.

Turning back to each other I raised my glass of wine to hers and said "To our adventure!" The Glasses chimed like two bells. "The bells of friendship a man once told me is what the French call that." I said as the chime faded. "I love it!" she exclaimed, and we raised our glasses again to enjoy the pleasant sound of friendship once more.

In reality, I felt, and I think Skylar did too, that our working friendship was growing into something more—something that neither of us wanted at this time; something that could get all tangled, sticky, and complicated; something that always seemed to happen when you least expected it and least wanted it. Neither of us was willing to bring this issue out into the open. Instead, we intoxicatingly danced around the issue, jousted with it, and feinted here and there, left and right. We spoke of nearly everything under the sun except how we felt about each other. Our eyes would meet and then we'd nervously glance away or hold long stares wrapped in smiles, not saying a word, just absorbing each other's internal impulse while sipping wine and nibbling on the last remnants of our cheese, cured meats and a little of the pasta dish. I had never met anyone like Skylar.

We were so different. If we were cloth, for example, we would have come from two entirely different bolts. Hers would have a refined, almost aristocratic feel, delicate by nature, yet durable by demand, embossed with a regal pattern, and hung or worn in the finest of households. My cloth would have come from a much rougher cut. It would be strong and reliable and would hold up well. The pattern on the cloth would be provocative and controversial, and although it might be respected or mildly admired by the finest households, things fashioned from this cloth would probably never be hung or worn frequently in those social circles. But that was okay by me. This fundamental difference provided me assurance that the two of us could never become embroiled in a romantic quagmire…"or could we," I thought to myself as her eyes drew me in. My thought was interrupted by Samuel's smiling face, for he had returned to our table asking "would you like anything else this evening?" Skylar and I looked at each other and both agreed we were finished and asked for the check.

We thanked him for a wonderful evening, his great service, delicious recommendations, and for sharing a little of his family history. "What are your names please?" he asked as Skylar and I stood to shake his hand goodbye. "I'm Skylar and this is Vince." "A pleasure to meet you Sky and Vince, I hope to serve you again one day." "I hope so too Samuel," I said, knowing more than likely I would never see him again. But I somehow knew the memory of this experience would be there forever.

• • •

I awakened the next day with aching muscles and a stiff neck. My first thought was that I had been bitten by a spider or a tick. I searched my body for an inflamed, red bite mark or tender area but thankfully found none. I decided the cause of my pains was the mattress made from hay that had matted into a flat hard surface and left me feeling sore all over. I paused and stared at the beautiful creation who was still fast sleep in the bed next to mine. Her seemingly pore-less complexion had a healthy glow. Her hair was curly and wild. Her lips were ripe and appeared as juicy as a Santa Rosa plum. She slept gently as she drew in deep, relaxed breaths, then, slowly and silently exhaled. "What have I done to deserve this?" I asked aloud, staring at the ceiling.

I was pulled from my reflective state by an obscene remark made by one passerby on the street to another. Even though the windows that overlooked the street were closed and the shades drawn, plates of glass were missing or shattered, leaving an incomplete barrier. Skylar awakened with a start and I saw terror in her eyes. "It's okay, Sky. Relax, it was outside, you're awake now," I told her. A look of recognition came over her taut facial muscles, as they one by one began to relax. I then placed kisses on her forehead and repeated reassurances between them.

Overnight we had grown closer. I now felt her presence deep within myself. I knew what was happening and realized my deep feelings would only increase the pain later, but no matter how hard I tried to rationalize my feelings in order to make them disappear, I could not resist falling for her. It was as if an avalanche had spilled forth from my heart, and nothing and nobody could stop it. The scariest thing, however, was that I wasn't sure how she felt about me. I mean, in past relationships I always wore my poker face, careful not to give away or show anything that could assist in figuring out how I felt about the girl. Yeah, it was not until she showed me her hand that I would reveal mine. I always knew how a girl felt about me before I told her how I felt. But today things were different. The game I had always been so good at had managed to lure me into revealing my hand first. The tricky part about it was that I didn't care if she knew I was head over heels for her. To the contrary, I was proud of it. For what I was feeling was pure and had no conditions or order. It was a driving force that propelled me almost without thought, fueled only by raw emotion. I was scared by the intense feeling of vulnerability that had descended. I wasn't *falling* in love. No, I was already there.

Chapter Five

Checking out, we thanked Ken for his hospitality and told him we were determined to be on Safari by dusk that day. He smiled and wished us good luck and made a few recommendations on how to accomplish this. He also warned us that there were a lot of "Safari con-artists" and to be wary of those promising "great adventure for little money." We said our goodbyes and were on our way.

By noon we found ourselves climbing the stairs of the Pan African House in search of a safari company. We heeded Ken's warning, and after speaking with several locals the majority agreed that the company we were looking for was housed in this building. The smell of old office spaces crept under the doors and into the large stairwell. By the third flight of stairs, Skylar's knees were aching as past running injuries reappeared. At the end of every set of stairs leading up was a black metal post with a decorative ball atop it. The black paint on the ball had been worn away, revealing a dull brass base. Sky used this to pull herself up the few remaining steps until we were at the office door we were looking for.

The office was straight out of a 1940s detective movie—from the single wooden desk and old black phone right down to the black and gold painted lettering on the glass pane of the wooden door that read "Savuka Tours and Safari Company." We sat in comfortable chairs in front of the antique desk. A three-blade ceiling fan rotated, sending a slight breeze our way as we began to extract the details of a possible safari. Behind the desk sat an amiable young businesswoman. She welcomed us and quickly engaged with the typical initial tourist small talk, including "What brings you two to Kenya?" Skylar shared an abbreviated version of our story with her and soon she was sharing her story with us. Afiya had recently graduated from Kenyatta University and this was her first job. Being a finance major, she keenly understood the importance of revenue generated by tourism and took pride in describing the safari in great detail to us. Her attractive facial features were smooth and dainty, her voice clear and steady. The woman in front of me represented the new breed, the future of Kenya—college-educated, with a keen sense of how important a booming tourist industry could be to the local economy. It was people like Afiya who would no longer allow the two-bit scams and con artists we were warned about to taint the Nairobi tourist industry. She did everything within her power to paint a clear picture of exactly what we would get for our money.

I had originally chosen this company because I'd heard it was operated by the Maasai people. The Maasai were icons of tribal Kenya who had managed to stay outside the stream of development within Kenya and were able to continue in the traditional occupation of cattle herding. All of this, of course, came up after I expressed our desire to see the famed Serengeti Plain from the unfettered perspective of those who lived there, and a tour company operated by the descendants of the original inhabitants of this mystical terrain sounded like it could provide us with just that.

Now here I sat before this beautiful and articulate woman who promised me a truly unforgettable journey to places where her ancestors had grazed cattle in the sweeping landscape of the Serengeti for centuries. By the time she had finished her soliloquy, her attempt to sell us a safari had become a wonderful synthesis of business and tradition, with the former thoroughly respecting the latter. Her sales pitch, which was delivered in excellent English, was a great example of how capitalism can work without spreading the infectious pus of exploitation.

Once again we found ourselves in the confines of a windowed passenger van. Finally the intense heat had begun to subside. Skylar and I sat on the first bench of the van, and for the first time on my visit to Africa, I had found a vehicle with an internal climate that agreed with me. Not too hot, not too cold. Not too many people, not a lot of noise, and I hoped this was an omen for things to come. We sat in silence as we rumbled down the road and out of the city.

The van carried eight people, all of whom would be part of this four-day adventure into the fabled Serengeti. We drove through the country on a route carving a southerly direction. I cannot recall whether the trip was scenic or not, but one thing that remains in my mind was that there always seemed to be something on the road that fully or partially obstructed it, whether it was rocks recently rolled free from adjacent hills, or tree-lined sections in which stretches of road were covered with fallen branches. As we drove, I found myself searching the roads for more of nature's artistic expressions. I could not recall having ever seen roads covered in such a meticulous fashion by fallen branches with leaves in various colors and stages of decay. Even the areas in which rocks had fallen to the road looked as if each stone had been purposefully placed. Had I been an artist, I surely would have captured those images.

I looked to my right, and fast asleep and curled up against me was Skylar. A slow trickle of drool descended in a translucent line from her pouting bottom lip to my shoulder. Laughing under my breath, I carefully took my bandanna and wiped her face.

An hour or so had passed when just up ahead in the roadway there lay a well-shaded area with a gas station, small store, and a vendor at a stall who peddled vegetable and chicken samosas and boiled rice. As we pulled in, I saw an old *Coca-Cola* ice chest.

I jumped from the van and took eager steps toward what I hoped would be a full chest of soda pop. Pulling up the lid, I revealed, to my delight, a cache of fizzy refreshments all neatly stacked according to flavor—*Fanta Orange, 7-Up,* and of course, one of the oldest ambassadors of the soda water industry, *Coca-Cola.* "Right on," I exclaimed, reaching into the cool depths and snatching a Coke. I popped the cap on the chest's built-in opener and consumed the contents of the cold, tiny bottle. There was the familiar burning in my throat and the tingle of the tiny bubbles in my nose as the liquid descended and helped to quench my intense thirst. Lowering the bottle, I noticed the white Coke logo was barely legible. In fact, the bottle was so scratched and nicked I was surprised it still held liquid.

I looked around to find six of the other seven people following my lead, all tipping a tiny bottle of caramel-colored liquid down their throats. I grabbed another for later on and paid the vendor at the stall.

On the other side of the gas station was a small store and gift shop. It looked interesting so I decided to investigate. Inside, the dirty walls were almost completely covered in carved woodworks that I assumed had been done by local artists. They were beautiful pieces of art, some depicting animals indigenous to the plains, others depicting the Maasai people. Some of the works had been done with a painstaking attention to detail, from the fine crow's-feet in the corner of someone's eyes right down to the veins on the backs of a subject's hands.

The shop smelled of stained wood and leather; in fact, many of the objects in the store had a unique odor. One object I picked up was a hollowed bull's horn with a leather top. "It can be used to store things," said the shop clerk. As I pried the top from the horn, a pungent odor of decaying flesh floated through the air. "Man, you were right, it certainly stored that odor well," I said, quickly putting it down.

Skylar was over by the sandstone carvings and had several

in her hands. "Which one do you think?" she asked, excited. "If I were to buy one?"

"The lion in your left hand. King of the jungle, that's the one for me," I said. Nodding in agreement, she put the others down and walked to the clerk. "I'll take this one, please."

We exited the shop arm in arm, and just then the man from the vendor stall stopped us just outside the door. He was trying to tell me something, but his English was so broken and my Swahili almost nonexistent, which left us unable to understand each other. "The bottle," a voice to my right volunteered. "He wants the Coke bottle back," he said, pointing at the extra Coke I had purchased for later. It was stuffed in the back pocket of my baggy Levis with the neck of the bottle exposed. The voice continued, "He wants you to drink the Coke here so he can keep the bottle." Despite the fact that I had already paid him for the deposit when I initially purchased the Coke, he wanted the bottle back to use it for something else or to double up on his deposit. Whichever it was, there was no way this guy was letting me walk away with it, and I couldn't blame him. At that moment I wanted to keep this bottle as an ageless reminder of this small but important lesson of how something as simple as a bottle of Coke symbolized so much more in their culture than in ours. This was why the bottles were so beat up, I thought to myself; they were used over and over again. Recycling was far more than a hobby in Africa; it was a way of life and I never wanted to forget that. I offered him double the amount he would have collected by merely returning the bottle. Not sure of what I was up to, he initially balked at my offer, but as soon as another man explained to him my reason and that the bottle represented more than just deposit money to me, he smiled and graciously told me to keep it. I carefully packed my reminder deep within the clothing inside my backpack and boarded the van.

• • •

"We are almost there," the driver announced. After many hours of travel and two flat tires, I was unexpectedly energetic and found myself eager to explore. Sky and the rest of the group shared my enthusiasm as we all anticipated getting the hell out of that van.

The camp consisted of ten or so two-person tents, a mess hall, a small kiosk that served as a store, a fire pit, and a single pipe jutting out of the earth where we could wash up. The water was not safe to drink, however. Encircled by a thick, protective barrier of brush and trees, much of the area was shaded, and the shabby tents were scattered. The mess and store resembled rickety shanties commonly seen in Hoovervilles during America's Great Depression. The tents were in only slightly better condition. They were made of drab green canvas, probably military surplus, that appeared no longer waterproof, because above each tent was an additional or auxilary roof made of tin or canvas supported by four poles cut from surrounding trees.

We filed out of the van and assembled in an open area near the fire pit. We stood anxiously awaiting instruction as our driver disappeared into the mess hall. Suddenly a monster of a man with a chef's hat appeared from the entrance where the driver had disappeared. "Welcome," he announced, ironically in a dense, unwelcoming tone. "I'm Jonathon, and I will be preparing your meals during your stay with us. Breakfast will be served from 7:30 to 8:30 a.m. Lunch from noon until 1:00 p.m., and supper will be a little longer between 5:00 and 6:30 p.m. I expect all of you to be on time. If you do not come at the proper times, go over to the kiosk and buy something to eat there. I can promise you, there will be nothing for you here." An uncomfortable silence fell over the crowd. A guy we drove in with slowly leaned toward me, Sky, and another passenger and whispered in an English accent, "What a pleasant chap." We all had a good chuckle then turned our attention back as Jonathon continued — "Now, first things first. Go and choose tents for

yourselves. Those of you who are single will have to pick a partner, and I don't want to hear any fuss. If you need bedding, it
can be hired from the kiosk for a hundred shillings. The blankets
are fifty shillings and an additional fifty as caution money,
which you will get back once the blankets are returned. However, they must be shaken clean of dust and folded. You do not
need to wash them. Failure to do this will result in our keeping
your caution money. Understood?"

"Yeah," "Sure," "Yes," the group sounded as one. I was waiting for him to give the order "Dismissed," but he just turned and
walked right back into the mess, his massive black arms swinging in confidence.

I wasted no time and scrambled to find a choice accommodation. I scouted for a few minutes before I found it. The tent
was located in a nice shaded area in a semi-secluded spot. The
tent had no holes, it reeked the least of oil, and the auxiliary roof
was in fine condition and supported by four sturdy logs, unlike
the others, which looked as if they had twigs supporting them.
"Our home for the next few days?" I asked Sky. "Perfect," Skylar
said, adding, "I'll arrange our bedding."

"Great," I replied. "I'm going to speak with our driver and
find out when our first outing in search of animals will be." As
I walked toward him, I noticed the silence had been broken by
nervous chitchat, giggling, and introductions among the members of the group. Excitement was everywhere.

The driver's name was Thomas and he also served as our
guide. He was a tall fellow with an angular body. He wore white
pants with a T-shirt and a light blue cardigan sweater with two
of the three buttons missing. As he spoke to other members of
our group, we learned he was middle-aged, and had a wife and
two little girls. He had been working as a driver for fifteen years-
ten as an overland truck driver and the last five with this company as a *game driver*. His candor in sharing with us a little about
himself helped to put our minds at ease. Some of the other mem-

bers of our group had shared with me the rumors they heard about game drivers. These rumors included stories of drunkenness, being robbed by them and then left in the middle of nowhere. As for Thomas, while he kept to himself, he seemed dependable and after all, he had been a truck driver for ten years like my grandfather, and my granddad was a stand-up guy. Plus, I had no solid reason to believe otherwise, only rumors.

I walked over. Thomas had just exhaled a long drag from his cigarette. He looked tired, so I didn't come right out and ask about the game drive; I just hinted at it. "Lot of driving!" I said. He took another drag off his smoke. "You must be tired," I added.

He nodded in agreement. "My name is Vince," shaking his hand while introducing myself.

"Nice to meet you, Vince," he responded in a slow, rough voice. This was going nowhere quickly. He was exhausted, and I couldn't straight up ask him, "Hey, Thomas, when are we going on our game drive?" without feeling guilty.

"Well, I'll be seeing you, Thomas," I said, ending the conversation.

"Okay, Vince, see you at dinner." I started to walk away when Thomas called from behind me, "Hey, Vince." I stopped and turned.

"Yeah?" I answered.

Walking toward me, he dropped his cigarette and crushed it beneath his boot. "Could you pass word to the others that immediately after dinner we will take our first game drive? If they could be prepared, it would assure us catching the last of the day's light, okay?"

A jolt of adrenaline shot through my veins. "Sure, sure I will," I agreed, barely able to contain my exuberance. "Thanks, Thomas." I turned and picked up my pace to spread the good news. "We go tonight," I exclaimed, as if conveying a long-awaited order to overanxious troops. Everyone was elated at the news. After all, the main point of our journey was to see the landscape and the famed animals of the Serengeti. However, much of what we would see depended on our driver and how many times he was willing to take us out. This was definitely a good sign.

That night we ate like locusts, devouring anything put before us. The food was simple, beans on toast, but it tasted good and there was plenty of it. Everyone engaged in conversation, trying to get to know one another. I sat next to the English guy's buddy. His name was Nicco and he hailed from Greece. He had just graduated from university and was taking a vacation before fulfilling his two years of compulsory military service. I could tell he was a little nervous, and he didn't agree with the military service policy. He felt he was wasting his time engaging in this endeavor, but still he had to do it. "They say it builds discipline and character. What if you already have discipline and character?" Nicco exclaimed. I didn't answer, but it was a fair question, I thought.

Nicco was of medium height and built like a college wrestler. He had a pointy beak, and his glasses rested nicely on it. He talked often and had a lot to say about the world. However, he also seemed to be frequently on the offensive, carrying a chip on his shoulder for no apparent reason. Maybe I was too quick to judge, but it seemed that the compulsory military service had him all riled up.

Peter, the Englishman, was from Kent. He, too, had recently graduated and was off to New York City for a job as a computer analyst. I asked, "Have you ever been to New York?"

"Raving mad, are they?" he responded.

"Well, let's just say it's a lot different from Kent. It is one hell of an experience. Come to think of it, I don't know of any other city in the United States, maybe even the world, that compares to it. One thing is for sure, though."

"What's that?" Peter queried.

"You will always have something new to do or see."

"Here, here, I'll drink to that," Peter declared. "To New York," we all shouted, hoisting and clinking our bottles of Coke together.

"Hey, by the way, is that your wife over there?" Nicco asked, looking in Skylar's direction.

"Yeah, I quite fancy her," Peter added.

"Listen up," I said with a look of intense seriousness. "If you so much as look at her, neither of you will be in any condition to finish this trip or any other trip, for that matter. Got it?" A silence fell over them and their faces went blank. All of a sudden I burst into laughter. Relief swept across their faces as their blank expressions turned to smiles.

"You bastard," Peter let out, "You really had me going there." We continued with a hearty laugh.

After dinner we all sat around drinking coffee and tea and sharing our experiences of Kenya. It was a very comfortable atmosphere, but I, like the rest, was eager to begin our safari.

Finally, Thomas stood from his chair and announced, "Please, everyone, quiet down. As you know, we will have our first game drive this evening, and I would like to know if everyone is ready to leave. If so, we should proceed because the sky at this time is quite beautiful."

Everyone looked around at each other, asking, "Are you ready?" Everyone answered in the affirmative. "Good, we will be off in ten minutes then," Thomas finished.

Skylar was now directly behind me, massaging my shoulders. "Shall we go?" she asked. "Sure, but first I would like you to meet Nicco and Peter."

"Peter, Nicco," she stated before shaking each man's hand. "It is a pleasure to meet the both of you." She then turned to me and said, "I'll meet you at the van." We stared at her as she sauntered away. "You've got your hands full with that one. She's got one hell of a grip, if you know what I mean, boyo," Peter said, changing his English accent to that of an Irishman.

"I warned ya," I shouted, firing a solid left into his chest. Nicco burst into laughter as I stood with my fists clenched. "There is more where that came from, my friend," I told him.

"All right, all right, I'm sorry," he apologized, smarting from the wallop.

"Now mind your manners," I said. "And that goes for you, too," I added, pointing at Nicco.

"Hey, man, I didn't say a word," he chuckled.

Chapter Six

I can no better describe one's first safari experience than I can one's first time in bed with a woman. I find them equally challenging to describe with any degree of accuracy. However, I can say this about both subjects with a fair amount of certainty: you will never experience anything quite like them again. With this aside, I can begin.

The light in the sky had never shown so beautifully as it did at that moment. It was just after sunset and right before darkness, and everything before us was illuminated with perfect clarity. The van traveled over tall grass and earth with uncommon smoothness. Out before us stretched miles of open land as far as the mind could imagine, and indeed one could have mistaken the earth for being flat.

Distinctive, flat-topped acacia trees punctuated the landscape, and bushes big and small filled in the spaces between the trees. Beautiful shades of brown, green, gold, and white were vivid to a degree I had never before experienced. Large rocks that had been pushed up from the cellars of time protruded from the earth's crust and made for beautiful geographical intrusions. The dark mountains in the background added the finishing touch as they stood visible in every direction. The moment at hand was intoxicating; we sat motionless, expressionless, and with eyes fixed upon the natural wonders surrounding us.

A narrow flow of water had cut a path through the terrain, and quietly standing near its edge were six hulking mammoths. Skillfully they reached down into the water with flexible trunks, then brought them up, and into their mouths the water gushed. Staring, I almost became lost in my own consciousness as everything was happening around me. Was it real? Only after their ears flapped and tails whipped around to swat annoying pests did I answer "Yes!" Their gray skin hung loose on their bodies, almost as if it were too big. Curved swords of ivory jutted forward gracefully from their jaws. It was painful to realize that while these beautiful, God-given gifts made them appear like royalty, they were also prized by humans, and those tusks plagued the splendid mammals like a death sentence.

As many fingers pressed multiple buttons, bulbs popped, shutters clicked, and film advanced. Everyone desperately tried to capture the image.

We continued on our search and came across a pair of giraffes with magnificent, starlike spots. They nipped at the foliage of the acacia trees, stopping only momentarily to look at us. Their long legs with big, knobby knees made them appear clumsy and slow, but I realized this assumption was false, for suddenly something startled the pair, a mother and her child. These awkward-looking mammals reached swift strides in a matter of seconds, and their heads locked in cadence with their long legs as they disappeared into the foliage.

Up ahead we reached a stretch of road that was completely obstructed by acres and acres of Thomson's gazelles, or tommies. "Watch this," Thomas said, driving toward them. As we inched closer and closer, the gazelles began to separate just enough to let us through, then re-clustered once we had passed; the van was like a steamer cutting through the ocean. We became immersed in a sea of horns, slipping deeper into the immense gathering. The process of opening and closing continued for miles. "I call this my Moses impression," Thomas said, taking a stab at being funny. It was the first time I saw him laugh, and we joined in.

The last of the day's light flickered out, and once again darkness reclaimed the earth. So we headed back to camp, the truck's lights illuminating the night. Finally we arrived and headed to our tents for a much-needed sleep.

• • •

I lay on my blanket with my eyes closed, but my eyes danced beneath their lids. My head was filled with so many images and thoughts it was ready to burst. I quietly left my bed and headed for the lone water pipe to wash. It was morning's first light, the darkness slowly relinquishing the earth back to the day. Africa sprawled out before me refreshed and cool. A ringing was in the air as insects sounded off, and a slight breeze carried the upbeat tune throughout the camp. Near the bushes behind the mess, a few large vultures scavenged a large heap of food waste left lovingly by Chef, while smaller birds looked on quietly as I approached the water pipe.

With a turn of the handle, the cool water poured into my cupped hands, and I splashed it onto my face, rinsing clean the sticky, sand like "sleep" caught in the corners of my eyes.

Opening my eyes, I saw a shadow standing before me in the dim light. It was Inga, a nineteen-year-old girl from Sweden. "You scared the hell out of me," I shouted as my body shuddered. "What are you doing up so early?" I asked with agitation in my voice.

"The same thing as you, I suspect. Sorry if I scared you," she offered in an apologetic voice.

Quickly changing my tone, I explained, "I'm sorry I snapped at you, Inga. I didn't sleep very well, so forgive me if I was short with you."

Inga was a sweet, shy girl. She had spent the summer living in a village near the Ivory Coast with an indigenous tribe, and she decided that before she returned home, she wanted to see as much of the continent as possible. She had blazed a path eastward across Africa and Kenya was her last stop. She was a big-boned girl and stood equal in height to a Land Rover. She had a round face with frigid blue eyes and long blonde hair with hints of white that she usually wore in a ponytail or bun. Her skin was slightly reddened by the sun from past months.

"Here you go," I said. Stepping back from the pipe, I realized with a sudden start that she was wearing only panties.

"Thank you," she responded as she began to wash her big but shapely body. At that point, I began to think maybe what I had heard about the Swedish having a very casual attitude toward sex and nudity was true. "I gotta visit that country some day!" I thought as I walked back to the tent, turning once to steal another glimpse.

"And where did you disappear to?" Skylar asked, kidding.

"I was just down at the water pipe, washing up." I paused. "Oh yeah, and then Inga showed up half-naked and I got a quick thrill. That was pretty much it," I added nonchalantly.

The bell indicating breakfast was being rung at a furious rate. On the tables sat cans of McCann's Irish Oatmeal. I poured the dry, weightless oats into my bowl and passed them over to Sky. Chef walked around ladling boiling water onto our oats. I watched them slowly expand and spent what seemed like the next twenty minutes blowing on them before they reached an edible temperature. I carefully shoveled the warm, soft spoonfuls into my mouth.

Again conversation consumed the table. Inga passed coyly in front of me. "Good morning, Vince!" she said. With a slight smile, I nodded my head, feeling a bit bashful. Thomas was speaking to Chef in Swahili, while Chef just moved his head in slow yes or no gestures but offered no words. Peter and Nicco were not at breakfast. They had stayed up late into the early-morning hours, drinking beer and talking. We all heard their muffled, tipsy speech and hearty laughter ring throughout the still darkness.

We left for a Maasai village in mid-morning, hiking about two hours over open ground, except for an occasional shade tree that we would stop to rest under. The heat was muggy, causing an uncomfortable, sticky layer of perspiration to form on our bodies.

We approached a dry riverbed and decided to follow it for a few miles because the lush vegetation that remained on the banks made for cooler passage to the village. Just as water began to appear, so, too, did the brush fence that encircled the village. We were finally there. As we entered, children ran about us and then ran off to announce our arrival. Thomas led as we passed through an opening between two mud huts called *tukuls*, that opened up into a commodious central area. We were told that this was the heart of their community, where traditional and ceremonial gatherings occurred, but for the moment it also hosted a central area for the tribe members to barter and sell items to tourists. Laid before us were numerous canvas sacks and blankets covered with beautiful necklaces, spears, clubs, and various containers fabricated from hardwoods, fresh leather, and sometimes bull horns. Each item had been crafted by a villager's hands and was now for sale to us.

Each member of the village who had items for sale sat on a blanket in silence until a visitor showed interest in a particular object on display. At this point, Thomas would step in and help facilitate the sale by establishing a price, and the visitor either accepted it or made a counteroffer. It was my experience that the haggling went back and forth until a deal was struck and a sale made. However, sometimes the price was not a monetary sum but an article of clothing, a watch, a hat, or other personal item possessed by the visitor. If this was the case, that item could only be acquired through trade. Nobody in my group went away empty-handed; in fact, many of us walked away with three or four beautiful works.

The Maasai people, as individuals, were works of art, but as a group they were an extraordinary exhibition. Their colorful attire was patterned in a way that I had never seen before. They wore presentations of vertical and horizontal stripes, stars and circles and squares within circles. The tincture used to color their apparel was equally impressive. Most pieces were bright and crisp; yellow, red, green, orange, blue, and white were distinctively clear. Even the dark shades like black and brown were unclouded and vivid. Dangling from their ears and worn gracefully around their necks was jewelry fashioned from beads in colors as vivid as those of their clothing. They were breathtaking to watch, and the only thing I could compare these beautiful patterns and colors to were traditional works produced by Native Americans.

Over to my right, a group of young Maasai women were sitting in the dirt. Each had a bald, perfectly shaped head glistening in the sun's light, skin that flowed like a layer of chocolate coating an apple flawlessly, captivating eyes, and bright smiles. "God, they are beautiful," I whispered to Skylar.

Thomas nudged me just hard enough to make my top ribs ache. "Look, Vince, over there," he said in a hushed tone. I looked up, and about twenty-five paces in front of me was the chief of the village. He was huskier in build than the rest of the men. He wore three pieces of colorful clothing that were, surprisingly, not as pleasant to look at as those I had seen so far. A long swath of fabric in a pink-and-white checked pattern was tied atop his left shoulder; it draped across his torso and around the right side of his body, then proceeded down to his ankles. The second piece of cloth was a green-and-white checked pattern, which was tied atop his right shoulder, ran across and around his left side and continued down to his ankles. A woven, brown leather belt was fastened around his waist to secure the garments in place. The final piece of cloth showed three fiery shades of red that ran in horizontal stripes, lightest to darkest. This piece draped over the chief's right shoulder and hung like a cape, covering the entire right side of his body. His hair was short and neat, and his teeth were dazzling white with a gap in the middle. His earlobes hung in loops of dark flesh, and he wore an elaborate necklace made from a marvelous array of multicolored beads. The finishing piece, however, was a quartz digital watch with a built-in calculator. No doubt it had been acquired in a trade. I personally did not see the sense in it. I mean, I had not looked at my watch once during the whole trip. In fact, I was debating whether I should pack it away for the remainder of the safari. After all, I was in the cradle of humankind, and one had no use for time out here; one just went on impulses and let nature take its course, or so I thought.

The chief squinted at the scene before him as he silently watched the exchange of our cash for the tribe's handcrafted goods.

Meanwhile, I quietly observed him. I wondered what kind of man and leader he was. I got to thinking about whether he had any children. If so, was he a good father? I suspected he was a gentle man because his hands were not the hands of a brute. His fingers were long and slender, almost feminine in appearance. His nails, like his teeth, were clean and had a dazzling glow. His stature was noble, yet his gestures and motions exuded compassion. His smooth, unlined face hinted that he rarely got angry. For if he did, anger creases, as I call them, would have been evident like the ones on my friend Steve's face back home. Steve spent so much time being angry that permanent creases had appeared at the top of his nose right between his eyes, and on his forehead directly above the corner of each eye. The chief's face showed no sign of that. I had an almost immediate liking for him, yet we had not exchanged a single word.

My thoughts scattered like startled birds as a group of village children gathered in front of the brush fence for a photo. The smallest one was making faces while shutting his eyes. This little guy was having a blast, taunting Sky as she tried to gain control of the photo. I laughed and thought, "Some things never change—no matter where you are." Most of the children were dressed in colorful Maasai cloth that draped over their shoulders, though two of the boys wore short-sleeved polo shirts—a subtle reminder to the elders of the growing Western influence through tourism.

Once the shutter clicked, the children ran toward Skylar with their arms outstretched and hands open. They wanted compensation for the photo. Skylar reached into her bag and pulled out a little something for each of them.

"That's going to be a great photo," Sky remarked, walking towards me.

"Yeah, but I don't think they liked posing too much," I responded. "In fact, some of the older boys looked at you with distrust."

"You're right," she conceded, "but did you see how their attitudes changed once I compensated them?" She added, "See, most people just take the photo and give nothing in return, but my mother taught me better manners than that." And her mother had, because when Sky reached into her bag she offered every person photographed a gratuity, and not only cash but things that were more personal and from her world. For instance, she passed out shirts from the university she'd attended, bandannas, candy bars, and even a pair of Ray-Ban sunglasses she carried as a spare in her backpack. She also handed out postcards depicting famous U.S. cities, including San Francisco, New York, and Washington, D.C., as well as ballpoint pens which one could not buy in the grasslands at that time. She gave it all with great pleasure. The children seemed to genuinely like her and not for the reasons that are obvious but because of her gentle soul. In fact, at the end of our visit, the children asked for a group picture—Skylar with the ten of them. This was a switch because it was usually the tourist who requested the photos. Watching her interact with these children was like watching a child's favorite toy come to life and play. I suspect she held their attention like no visitor had previously. I even noticed the elders who normally gazed at the newcomers with ice-cold glances thawed under Skylar's brightness, and they cracked smiles as they watched her playing with their grandchildren. There she stood, cradling a child with each arm and more gathered around her knees, reaching up, wanting to be held next.

I reminded myself, as I had done so many times previously, what a lucky guy I was.

"Vince," she called out, "come with me," as she held an extended hand open.

"Where are we going? " I asked as I clasped my hand around hers.

"One of the children invited you and me into his parents' home."

When we reached the family's hut, we both bent down to make it through the tiny entryway. Just inside, all standing in a row, was the boy, his younger brother, and his mother and father. "Hello," Sky and I said to them, bowing our heads to show respect. They smiled and did the same. Each boy grabbed one of Sky's hands, pulled her forward, and waved me in too.

The dwelling was small and dark and had a dank, fetid odor that hung in one's nostrils. It was the smell of raw human existence without the luxury of interior plumbing— an odorous reminder that we, too, are animals. There was only one opening to enter or exit by, and two or three porthole-size windows where a few sun rays poked through. I assumed the openings were kept small in order to protect against the penetrating midday sun. I cannot recall seeing a single possession; no pots, pans, dishes, blankets, pillows, or even clothes besides the cloth they had on their backs. The roof was low, and we hunched down as we took no more than six steps forward. Before us on the hard dirt floor were four mats on which the family slept. We took a few more steps and the boys pointed to a fire pit where the family prepared and cooked meals.

Other details have escaped my memory and are lost to time. However, one detail that will forever remain with me is the pride the two boys took in showing us where they lived. I knew this was a rare occurrence, for as we were walking to the village, Thomas had instructed us to stay together in the center of the village. He said that by no means should we wander into any of the tukuls without being invited, and now here we were, inside the humble living quarters of our two young hosts and their parents.

We emerged from the small opening into the brightness of the day. We were temporarily blinded, and our backs ached from leaning over so much. Skylar stretched and I shaded my eyes as they readjusted to the light.

That evening at dinner, Thomas announced that we would have a special night of entertainment: The young Maasai men from the village would perform a ceremonial dance for our enjoyment. We all broke into applause because we knew Thomas had arranged this personally; it was not originally part of the safari. "Three cheers for Thomas," Peter said, raising his dinner fork. "Hip, hip, hurrah! Hip, hip, hurrah! Hip, hip, hurrah!" we shouted, our voices carrying through the undisturbed night air like a telephone wire, filling the countryside with laughter and cheering.

I broke from the group and walked over to the little kiosk nestled at the far end of camp. The old shopkeeper, who knew my face, saw me approaching, put down his magazine, and quietly pulled a box of English shortbread biscuits from the shelf above his head and two bottles of Coke from the crate on the floor. I always had to wait for him to add up the cost. On some nights it was one hundred shillings, other nights it was one hundred and fifty. It didn't matter, though, because he always had a smile on his face and remembered what goodies to retrieve for me. In fact, the previous night it went around camp that the shortbread was all gone, but he waved me over when no one else was watching and stealthily handed me the last box. For some reason, whether it was the fresh, unpolluted air, the hours spent driving and hiking the grasslands, or sleeping in tents under the stars, my appetite for sweets seemed to have increased tenfold. Our personal supply had been largely exhausted by midday on the second day, and Sky had selflessly given our remaining bars of chocolate to the Maasai children. So the only place to get sweets was the kiosk, and it didn't have chocolate bars, just the little shortbread biscuits. In the center of camp, I could see Thomas and the others setting up seats around a large campfire. I quickly stashed my snacks and hustled over to help. "We need more seats!" Chef growled. "More seats!" So Nicco, Thomas, and I grabbed a large old log that was just outside the mess and dragged it over by the fire. "A little closer...no, back it up...no, too close...that's it, right there," Chef said, supervising as the three of us strained. The log may have been old and dried up, but it weighed a ton. "A bench," Thomas announced as he sat, checking to make sure it was comfortable. Chef disappeared as usual into the mess.

We were already halfway through the safari and I still hadn't figured out Chef. Nobody knew if he was married, had kids, nothing. Even when I asked Thomas, who seemed to be the closest to him, what Chef's story was, he just shrugged and said, "He is a good cook, his name is Christian, and the rest, my friend, is a mystery." This wasn't hard to believe, because from day one, he'd gone out of his way to put fear into everyone, so nobody said a word to him except for an occasional "Thanks" when he ladled food onto a plate. Other than that, it seemed clear he didn't want to talk to anyone. Additionally, Chef was always pissed off about something, so it made it easy for us to not want to even try and engage him in conversation. He was pissed that his knives were old and dull. He was pissed that he had to cook the same meals for every group that came on safari. He was pissed if you didn't show up for meals during designated times, which rarely happened, but if it did, and you were dumb enough to go into the mess and ask for something to eat, he would tear into you and take great pleasure in doing it.

Everything about life seemed to anger Chef, and it took very little to set him off; just waking up in the morning would do. He was a scary-looking dude to boot. At about six feet four and 230 pounds, he made you want to stay out of his way. Thomas had said that after every meal, he would see Chef finishing off all the remaining food. I think this was why he made so much of it. This was what also kept him about two sizes bigger than any of the local men I had seen in this area. To add to his already intimidating presence, he nurtured a thick black beard and had a gleaming bald head. This, of course, was seen only on occasion, since he wore his chef's hat most of the time. I wouldn't have been surprised if he slept in it. I think he would have been pissed if he knew we called him Chef instead of Christian. But what the hell, it fit. That tall, white gourmet chef's cap was soiled from years of wear and while what he was preparing for us was far from gourmet, to his credit, it was good, it was hot, and that was all that mattered.

By now I could feel the heat radiating from the campfire. The entire group had congregated around the flames, speaking in hushed tones. Between the game drives and the hike to the Maasai village, everyone was pretty well tuckered out.

Slowly our guests emerged out of the darkness. They quietly gathered, keeping their distance out of shyness, waiting for Thomas to return. We took the initiative in making them feel welcome by smiling, waving, and shaking some hands. They drew closer, and I could make out twenty-five people in total. They were young, male, the majority over six feet tall, and they all seemed a bit nervous.

Thomas approached, asking us to take a few steps back to make sure there was enough room for our young tribesmen.

Each held a spear, and now they formed a line and walked, one after the other, into the center of our gathering and around the fire. Forming an interior circle, they continued to walk around the flames as a low, mumbled chant began to build. Movements became flowing, and after a few moments, individuals broke into standing leaps, one after another. Their synchronicity was flawless. The last time I had seen something this flawless in execution was watching a Marine Corps silent drill platoon back home as a kid. The young Maasai used only the power of their feet and ankles to launch themselves six to eight feet into the air while continuing in a flowing, chanting circle. It was an amazing sight, especially since the torso and arms of each one who leapt into the air remained perfectly straight. I know this sounds impossible, but I, as well as eight others, witnessed these agile beings cheat gravity. It was even more impressive when they began to leap in unison and continued to move flowingly around the circle of fire.

The air was filled with a rhythmic, regular cadence as their feet hit the sun-hardened soil. Their voices were an orchestra. One person would shout out a phrase and the rest would respond, producing a booming harmony. The pace was mesmerizing, and it all looked mystical and ancient. The white smoke and crackle of the large flames added to the powerful display. With incredible endurance, they continued for nearly forty-five minutes. By the time it was over, not one of them was breathing hard. However, beads of sweat had formed like raindrops on their heads and ran down into their eyes and mouths.

We applauded the performance, which I thought strange, but I joined in the clapping. Still, it made me feel uncomfortable to think that this dance symbolized something special to these people and was probably most often performed only for fellow Maasai, although tonight it had been turned into entertainment for white people. It just didn't seem right. I voiced my opinion to Nicco and Peter, but they looked at me as if I had gone mad.

"You think too much, man; just enjoy it," Nicco told me. Maybe I did, but at least *I* was thinking, I thought in silence.

Just as quietly as our guests had arrived, they departed. Only a handful remained, and one of them, a very old man, was speaking to Thomas. As the old man spoke, he began to stare past Thomas, who then turned, trying to see what had caught the old one's attention. His gaze fell on me. "Ah, the Inquisitive One," he said, using a nickname he'd given me because of the endless questions I asked. "What is on your mind this evening, my friend?" I smiled and felt the blood rush to my cheeks. "Come, sit with us and meet a real Maasai warrior," Thomas said, turning to the old man and translating what he had just told me. The old man got the biggest kick out of that and started to laugh. I guess Thomas then went on to tell him of my reputation for asking "Why?" or "How come?" for the old one laughed uproariously, then settled into a serious mood. He spoke and Thomas began to translate. "When I was a young man of your age, we, the Maasai, still had a reputation as fierce warriors. Nothing scared us, not even the mighty lion. The English used guns to kill lions; we killed lions using only spears. A warrior has to be up close to use a spear with accuracy and effectiveness.

"While this century was still young," he continued, "my grandfather grazed cattle at watering holes that today are underneath the paved streets in Nairobi City. He had witnessed the building of the railway that began in Mombasa and stretched deep into Uganda. Indian slaves by the tens of thousands were used to build a railway they would never even be permitted to ride.

"My grandfather, along with many of my people, died during a famine. My father survived and struggled to improve life for himself by taking up the raising of cattle, which was at that time a traditional way of making a living. Back then, our cattle were free to roam and graze as they pleased. Today it is much different. Both my people and our cattle were displaced once the game reserve was established. With a single stroke of a law-maker's pen, much of the land was taken away, put off limits. We were forced to accept settlement programs that preached of land ownership and raising crops, both of which are alien concepts to the Maasai. Even our treasured ceremony to become a warrior, *a morran*, was affected by these land restrictions." He stopped talking at this point and looked down at the ground as if the memories of what once was were becoming too painful to recall. After a moment of silence he composed himself and said, "Today we are a people who struggle to keep alive the very identity and traditions that have made us who we are. As times change, we try to remain the same. Of course, in the world of today, this is impossible, and so we, too, change. I fear that as we continue to change, we will one day not remember who we once were. For now, we continue to raise cattle and dress and perform the traditions of ceremony, much like our ancestors did, but in time these, too, will pass into history."

He then stood, using a staff to support his long, frail frame, and told me, as Thomas strained to translate, "It is good to want to know and learn. May you never lose that instinct, but remember to always seek the truth within those things."

I made my way back to the tent. Poking my head through the flaps, I found Skylar reading by flashlight. "Come with me," I said. She slipped into her boots and appeared in the opening. "Where are we going?" she asked, pushing her wild hair from her face. I pointed up. Above us, far into the darkness, burned the white candles of heaven. Like everything I had seen on the grasslands, the stars, too, showed better and brighter than I had ever seen them. Long white trails from dying stars filled the night.

"Quick, make a wish," Skylar urged.

"You too," I shot back as the shooting stars carried our wishes, disappearing into oblivion. We stood face to face, locked in an embrace, watching the heavenly procession. A feeling of well-being came upon me, as if I had come in from the cold to a warm glow. I wanted this feeling to never leave. I was once told by a friend that our whole lives are spent searching for the safety and comfort we once experienced in our mother's womb, and for a fleeting moment, I believed I had found it.

We returned to our tent, zipping it up securely until morning. Our lamp was the last to be extinguished that evening.

Boarding the van the following morning, we set out in a direction we had not traveled before. Suddenly, the brakes screeched to a grinding halt. The road ahead was blocked as a herd of cattle crossed the narrow road. We patiently waited until the last of the animals had passed. Bringing up the rear were two Maasai shepherds, both brimming with wide smiles and waving to thank us for stopping. I stuck my hand out the window and gave them a peace sign, which they both returned and held until we drove out of sight.

A group of vervet monkeys looked as if they were playing tag. Their little black faces fringed by white hair displayed excitement as one chased after the others until it touched one; then it was the tagged monkey's turn to be "it."

In the distance, on a huge rock, rested a pride of lions. Thomas, noticing this, adjusted his course and was now heading directly toward them.

Before us rested nature's royalty. The lions were absent, but the lionesses and cubs lay in a semicircle, lazily taking in the cool morning. Their laziness was apparently due to having just eaten a morning meal. A wide trail of fresh blood stained the face of the rock and slowly trickled down to collect in a pool on the dirt. "Look," Thomas said, pointing to the vultures gathering in the air above the rock. "The carcass must be somewhere on top of the rock," he added, and he maneuvered the vehicle around to get a gander.

I stared at the vultures, wondering if they ever got tired of sloppy seconds. They always had to wait for the lions to depart before they could swoop down for a bite. It was an echo of human societies' construction: the offering of scraps and drippings from the royal table to the peasants or lesser beings. On the other hand, the vultures had it pretty easy. While the lions did all the work chasing the prey, cornering it, and killing it, the vultures merely circled overhead. They ate pretty well for scavengers. And let's face it, the meat left around the bones is the best part, and they knew it.

Thomas grew increasingly frustrated as his attempt to see what the lions had killed bore no fruit. The rock was more like a small mountain and our sight was obscured by its height, so the carcass remained concealed.

Suddenly, an ominous roar exploded. It had built deep within, traveled up the esophagus, and exploded powerfully out of the lion's gaping mouth. "A King is near," Thomas warned, but no one could see it. Thomas said, "When a human hears a lion's roar, you will notice it first registers in one's sphincter as one feels the muscles tighten, and then it proceeds up into the back of one's throat with a slight tickle." It sounded nothing like the roar of a lion in captivity; no, this was much more terrifying, especially when you could not see the roaring lion. Once again a thunderous roar filled our ears, but nothing filled our eyes. Like the carcass, the lion was concealed somewhere, either atop the rock or hidden in the thick brush located at the rear of its base. Not being able to see him created a sense of excitement. No doubt each of us had constructed in our mind what he looked like. Probably he was a seasoned old warrior who had defended his pride on more than one occasion. He was letting us know he knew we were near, and if need be, he would defend what was his. Unfortunately or maybe luckily, we never saw him despite our search.

The last morning in camp was a dreary one. Skylar and I quietly shook and folded our blankets and returned them to the kiosk. The old guy behind the counter handed me back my caution money and said good-bye.

"Good-bye," I replied. "And thank you for your kindness." I handed him back the fifty shillings.

Chef, just like the first time we cast our eyes upon him, stood in the doorway of the mess. I waved and shouted, "Good-bye, Christian," expecting nothing.

Then a miracle: "Good-bye, Vince," he said. I stopped dead in my tracks and turned to say more, but he had already disappeared into the mess.

Sky was sitting on a metal stool outside the tent. "You'll never guess who said good-bye to me," I told her.

"Chef," she replied, stealing the thunder from my surprise. I paused for a moment, trying to figure out how she knew.

"But can you believe it?" I asked as I picked up our bags.

She answered, "You have an infectious zest for life that seems to grow on people, and that's why I love you." And then she kissed me. For the second time that morning, I froze in my tracks due to words I had not expected to hear.

"What did you say?" I asked, hoping she would say it again and hadn't made a mistake.

"That is why I–love–you!" she said, enunciating those three words slowly and clearly. I just stood there with a stupid grin on my face. "You're silly," she said, walking over and kissing me again. "Let's get going; everyone is gathered by the bus waiting for us."

We all promised to write one another, and so began the process of exchanging addresses. However, in the back of my mind, I knew more than likely most would not, regardless of the possibility presented by the exchange of information. I knew that once we returned to our worlds, we would abandon this briefly adopted one.

Driving away, I watched as the huge thunderheads rolled in just as swiftly as a squadron of B-24 bombers I had seen in an old Movietone Newsreel, their thunderous roar filling the air as if saying goodbye. As I gazed through the tiny back window of the van, I realized I was leaving a place I would likely never see again. I was saddened by this thought, but I was also excited at the adventure that lay just ahead in Tanzania.

PART II

Chapter Seven

As soon as we were back in Nairobi, Sky and I found ourselves at the window of a station agent trying to get a train out of there. Unfortunately, there was no international service, so we would have to take a train partway and then a bus the rest of the way to Dar es Salaam. No such luck.

"I'm sorry, the tickets are sold out on all trains heading in that direction," said the agent.

"There aren't two seats available on any train heading toward Dar?" Skylar asked urgently.

"Miss, didn't you hear me the first time? The tickets are sold. There is no room," he repeated sternly.

"Thanks." She shied away but then stopped. "Excuse me," she said, interrupting his calculations. "What is the next best way to get to Dar?" she queried.

"Try a bus," he responded dryly.

"Which number? Which bus? Where is the bus station?" I questioned, growing frustrated with his lack of assistance.

Not raising his eyes from the paper he was concentrating on, he said, "All right, where is the bus station? Sir, I do not deal with buses, only trains."

"Thanks for nothing, pal," I growled.

"You're welcome, sir," he responded nimbly, angering me further.

He could have at least told us that there was no proper bus station. No, the buses were all privately owned and housed in buildings of their own, not in one central station. There were so many of these little bus outfits, we didn't know which one would provide us with reliable service. I mean, each outfit had a catchy little name and advertisement since it seemed each was trying to outdo the next—luxury bus, luxury express bus, super-luxury express bus. However, all the buses looked pretty much the same—dirty, overcrowded, and they all got you to the same place in the same amount of time, barring a breakdown. Still, like typical Americans, we paid a little more and went with the super-luxury express bus with a TV and air-conditioning.

Our trip to Dar was divided into two parts. First we would go to Arusha, Tanzania, and spend a night there, and then go on to Dar, with arrival promised during daylight hours. This was good, for we had no idea where Dr. Goodall's house was located.

We waited on a bench as rows of buses idled, emptying black exhaust into the already clouded air. The area was vibrating from activity. People gathered in the streets, on the sidewalks, anywhere there was a bus. Everyone was anxious to get where they were going, or excited about returning from where they had been. Smiles curved, hands shook, lips kissed, and eyes teared.

A boy approached with a box in one hand and a small, three-legged, wooden stool in the other. "Shoe shine, mister?" he asked with bright eyes. Having my shoes shined was the last thing I wanted then, but I didn't have the heart to turn him down. "What the heck," I said.

"Is that yes?" he asked, not sure of my slang.

"I'm sorry, that means yes," I explained, pulling my legs from under the bench and stretching my boots in the kid's direction. He set his stool down, and the uneven legs caused him to lean slightly back. He put the box of polishes by his left foot. He examined my shoe, rummaged through his box, picked a few bottles, held them up to the sun for a closer look, and chose the bottle containing the color closest to my boots. He then proceeded to wash my boots with a cloth that he dipped in a bucket of water. Unfortunately, the water was dirtier than my boots; he really didn't remove the dirt, he just moved it around some.

Unscrewing the bottle, he carefully swabbed on the concoction, and a smile came across his face; it was an exact match. I was impressed. After letting the color dry, he buffed my boots to a nice shine. My boots really looked great. "*Asante*," I said.

"You like?" he asked.

"Very much," I responded.

"Do you have any more I can shine?" he asked.

"No," I answered, then thought again, looking around for Sky. "Go ask that woman over there," I said, then sat back and watched the scene unfold. He ran up to her and tugged on her pants. She turned to see the little guy. Smiling, she knelt down to talk with him. She nodded her head in agreement, and he eagerly put his stool down and started to work. Upon finishing, the little guy turned and pointed at me. She looked over and saw me, I waved, and she replied by blowing me a kiss. That was the only time I wished I had a camera.

Finally our bus was clean and ready for boarding. We filed onto the old school bus and took our bench-style seats. I sat near the window so Sky could stretch her legs into the aisle. Her knees were really sore, and I knew she wasn't looking forward to this long, cramped ride, but she never complained.

With the bus driver's strong jerk of a lever, the doors squeaked closed. The driver turned the key, igniting the diesel in the pistons, and with a sticky shift into first gear and a release of the brake, we began our trip to Dar es Salaam.

After two days and sixteen hours of travel, our bus dropped us in Dar, and into the pitch of night and not during daylight as planned. We didn't mind though; we were just happy to be off that bus! Outside the air was thick with smoke, and I coughed as we stepped from the bus into it. As I walked around to the rear, our luggage, along with the luggage of other passengers, was being untied from the roof rack. The driver, on top of the roof, was now hanging over the edge with one hand on my bag and the other on a rail in an attempt to lower my suitcase to my extended hands. He released it a foot from my grasp, but its awkward weight caused me to lose my grip, and the suitcase landed with a thud on the brown, flour-like soil.

On the other side of the bus, Sky was waiting for her luggage. I walked over, dusting off my bag, and I could tell she was relieved that she had not placed her suitcase on the roof. No, her bag was lucky enough to have found its way into the storage belly of the bus, where it was protected from the harsh sun and dust. However, once she retrieved it, a pungent smell of gas and oil stuck to the outer shell of her suitcase, and she hoped it had not penetrated through to her clothing. I could live with a little dust, but smelling like a petrol station—that would be hell.

Kerosene lamps held by individuals blinded us as we made our way off the street and onto the sidewalk, or should I say what was supposed to be a sidewalk, for it went on for only ten feet or so. "Where do we go from here?" I asked.

Pulling her hair back into a bun, she answered, "I say we find a telephone and call this number." She unfolded a small piece of yellow paper with a sequence of numbers and "Dr. Jane Goodall" written underneath.

"I thought you lost that," I said.

"I thought I had, but while I was digging through my clothes to see if the smell of the case had absorbed into my clothes, I found the number hiding by the hinges of my case. Pretty lucky, huh?"

"I'll say," I agreed. Without that number, we pretty much had no way of getting in contact with Dr. Goodall. For some reason or another, Jane never gave Skylar her address, just the phone number, and Skylar thought she had lost it while on safari so we were both relieved that Sky had found it. Now we just needed a phone and we'd be in business.

Our search for a phone brought us to a small motel. Walking in, I noticed there was a restaurant on the second floor, and I made a mental note to get something to eat. The lobby was tidy and well lit. The man behind the counter had an inviting smile, and immediately he asked, "May I help you?"

"Yes," Sky answered. "May I use your telephone to make a call to a local number in Dar?" He paused and looked at us from head to toe. I was wearing a ripped pair of jeans, a T-shirt, and boots, and Sky was in a pair of U.C. Berkeley sweatpants, a T-shirt, and running shoes. Both of us were dragging from the journey and were covered in a light layer of dust. Nonetheless, he said, "Of course."

Sky made the call while our courteous attendant made conversation with me. "Have you come far?" he queried.

"Yes, from Nairobi by bus," I answered.

"All by bus, did you say?" he wondered.

"Yes, unfortunately the trains in this direction were all full," I said, breathing out heavily.

"Did you know the tracks are all linked? You could travel all the way from Nairobi to Dar by rail, but the countries cannot reach agreeable terms for an international service. It is a shame," he finished, shaking his head with disappointment.

"Oh, taking a bus was all right. It was an adventure. We got to stay in Arusha for a night. Yes, it was quite nice, actually," I told him.

He just looked at me oddly, as if I were crazy for having made the best of it. "Ah, to be young," he proclaimed with a smile, then turned to check on how Skylar was doing. "Are you getting through okay, love?" he questioned.

"No, I keep getting a ringing sound, and then it just goes dead," she told him with agitation in her tone.

"Come now, let me try." He grabbed the receiver and dialed the numbers slowly on the black rotary. "You're right," he confirmed. "The line is not working properly."

"Great," I said, rolling my eyes. Skylar thanked him and offered some shillings in return for his kindness, but he refused, claiming it was a free call. "Good-bye," I said, offering him my hand.

"Where will you go?" he asked.

"I guess we'll spend the rest of the evening flagging down taxis until we find a driver who knows where Dr. Goodall lives? She is quite famous, so it shouldn't be too hard finding her house," I explained.

"What's her name?" our new friend questioned.

"Dr. Jane Goodall," I said, crossing my fingers. He looked up, squinted his eyes, and by his actions I could tell he was in deep thought. He remained silent for a matter of seconds, then his eyes relaxed and his head lowered, "I'm sorry, I'm afraid I don't know her," he apologized. "I take it she is American?"

"No, she's British," I responded. He was silent, and I think even a bit disappointed in himself for not being able to help us. "No worries," I said. "Thanks anyway for trying and for letting us use your phone."

As we were about to exit the lobby, we heard, "Why do you not stay here for the night? I have a nice room available, then you could have a fresh start in the morning with the sun's light."

I looked at Sky. "It makes sense," I said.

"Yeah, he's right, it is much harder at night, plus I'm exhausted," she said, setting her suitcase down.

I turned to our host. "Okay, we'll stay," I said, setting my dusty case on the floor. "Oh, by the way, I noticed a restaurant upstairs. Is it open?" I asked. He looked at his watch. "Half past ten," he mumbled to himself and said, "I'm sorry, the cook has gone home, but if you want something simple—"

I interrupted, "Like an omelet and toast?"

"Like an omelet and toast," he said, chuckling at my enthusiasm. "My wife will make it for you."

"Thank you, sir," I said, shaking his hand as if I hadn't eaten in a month.

We brought our suitcases into the room we were given and left them near the door. The room, like the lobby, was neat and well lit. "Look, we have our own shower," Skylar said gleefully as she walked into the bathroom. "And it's a real one with an en-closure, hot and cold faucets, and a genuine showerhead," she added, as the excitement grew within her voice. It felt strange to be so excited about something so common in the States. I mean, fresh hot and cold running water brought into our houses by pipes traveling miles underground to the source, showers en-abling people to cleanse themselves as often as they saw fit, and sanitary latrines that carry our waste miles and miles away from us to sanitation plants in order to prevent disease were all re-markable conveniences that I had taken for granted so many times back home. But here, now, I noticed a growing apprecia-tion for these luxuries. My grandparents would be proud.

The room filled with steam from the shower as I relaxed and let the warm streams of water run against my back and neck. Looking down, I watched a tainted flow of water travel down my leg and into the drain. "This is heaven," I thought, as the streams ran against my face.

With the windows open, the pleasant aroma of food drifted in and taunted our ever-increasing hunger. We dressed quickly and went upstairs to eat. Opening the door, we saw there wasn't a soul in sight. On a table located almost in the center of the din-ing room sat a feast fit for royalty. The innkeeper's wife had pre-pared three omelets—plain, cheese, and some type of vegetable one for Skylar. In a basket were freshly toasted slices of bread wrapped in cloth. Everything was still hot as steam escaped from each item. Fresh orange juice was served in a glass pitcher, and tea sat steeping in a porcelain kettle. Sky and I looked at each other in disbelief at the efforts that had been taken to pre-pare our meal.

A tiny woman wrapped in an apron appeared from behind a swinging door. "Come, sit. Eat before it cools," she com-manded with a smile, sensing our appreciation. We gladly did what she instructed. I sat quickly, salted my plain omelet, and added a touch of hot sauce. The first bite was heaven, and my taste buds almost ached with relief. The toast was golden brown and crunched under every bite taken. The orange juice was sweet and smooth with little acidic taste. Topping off our feast, we sat back in our chairs and poured a cup or two of tea from the warm kettle. I added a few teaspoons of honey, which looked more like molasses due to its dark color. The warm, sweet liquid coated my throat and helped to soothe the irritation of having inhaled diesel fumes from our long journey.

I looked around at the neatly situated tables, ten in number, all carefully covered in different-patterned cloths. Each one had a small vase containing a single fresh flower that filled the air with a sweet fragrance.

Our friend from the lobby came up. "How was your meal?" he asked. Sky and I searched for words, but it was our expressions that told him we were quite satisfied. "Excellent," he said. "Now, after a good rest you will be ready to find this Dr. Goodall."

We rose from our chairs and pushed through the swinging door and into the kitchen to thank our gracious cook, but she had already gone. Our friend was picking up our dishes, and we asked where his wife had gone. "She's off to bed," he answered. I began to help him gather the plates and brought them to the sink.

"I'll wash the dishes," Sky announced.

"Do not be silly, you are my guests. What kind of host would I be if I made you wash the dishes?" he stated.

"Are you sure?" we asked.

"I'm sure," he smiled.

"Okay then, good night," we said as the door swung closed behind us.

"Good night, my friends," he replied. "Sleep well."

I awoke the next morning with the warm rays of the sun's light beating upon my face. It was just past seven as I lay in bed staring at the rotating blades of the ceiling fan. Skylar had been up for a while, getting sick in the bathroom. She had begun to feel ill during the final leg of our trip to Dar, but she'd managed to fight it off until five that morning. "Are you feeling any better, Sky?" I called into the bathroom.

"No," she said firmly. "I think those chicken samosas I ate at the rest stop gave me food poisoning!"

"I don't think so, because I ate them as well, and I feel great," I told her.

"Thanks for rubbing it in," she replied in a defeated tone, then turned to put her face back above the porcelain bowl.

"Oh, I didn't mean it that way, I was just—"

Sky interrupted my explanation with the sound of visceral contractions as she leaned further into the bowl, vomiting.

"I'll just go to the lobby and check out, okay?" I said, knowing full well it was moments like this when one wanted privacy. She waved me to go while her head remained over the toilet.

Outside, the air was still. I knew the day was going to be a hot one. It was almost eighty degrees and not quite eight o'clock. Opening the lobby door, I saw our new friend doing some sort of paperwork. "Good morning," I said.

"Ah, good morning. I trust you slept well?" he asked.

"Yes, exceptionally well. That was the most comfortable bed I've slept in since leaving home. You run a very nice establishment here," I told him. He nodded graciously to thank me.

"And where is your beautiful companion this morning? Still sleeping?" he asked.

"I'm afraid she's feeling a bit under the weather this morning. It's her stomach," I said. He looked at me with fright. "Oh, no, I assure you it wasn't your food," I explained, and a look of relief came over his face.

"I will have one of my staff go to the pharmacy and get some stomach medicine right away," he said. Then he called out, "Joseph, Joseph." A young boy no older than ten came quickly to the lobby. His sweaty appearance indicated that he was already working hard in the morning sun. They spoke in Swahili, and Joseph departed, passing me with a breeze. "I'll have him bring it to you when he returns. It should only take a few minutes; the pharmacy is just down the way," he explained.

"Is this guy for real?" I thought to myself. I mean, I believe in being hospitable to your guests, but this guy literally treated us like we were family. The next thing I expected was for him to tell us our room was on the house. Well, he must have tapped into my thoughts because as I opened my wallet and asked about the bill for the meal and the night's stay, he just grabbed my hands and wallet softly and said, "Please, you are my guests, and you are now my friends, and I do not expect friends to pay." He gave me a sincere, penetrating glance.

"I can't," I stated.

"You must!" he insisted. There was silence.

"I can't," I repeated. More silence descended upon us, and I could tell from his eyes he was not giving in, so I did. "Thank you, sir, your kindness is overwhelming."

"Please call me John," he said.

"Thank you, John, very much. I will always remember your generosity," I told him with that same look of sincerity he had bestowed upon me. I shook his hand for a third and final time. "I do not mean to be rude, but I must check on Sky," I told him.

"Okay, my friend, travel safe," he finished. I turned to exit when John called out, "Excuse me, Vince? One more thing..."

"What's that?" I asked.

"The only thing I ask is that you please tip Joseph for his trouble," he said.

"You're a good man, John, to look after your workers. Of course I'll tip him," I assured him.

"Thank you and welcome to Tanzania!" he shouted as I left the lobby.

Skylar's skin was as white as the sheets we had slept on. Her eyes were sunken and her lips were dry and cracked, but surprisingly, she was in high spirits. "This thing is really kicking my ass!" she stated with a smile as I entered the room.

"It's good to see you smile again," I told her.

"I'm all packed and ready to go," she said. "Is everything paid up?"

"You bet it is," I said and sat down on the bed with her to explain. "As a gift for being his new friends, you know the guy in the lobby, John? He gave us the meal and the room for nothing."

"You're kidding," she said.

"Nope, it was all free. Can you believe it? In fact, he even sent one of his staff to the pharmacy to buy you a bottle of stomach medicine," I said.

"You're kidding," she repeated in disbelief.

"It's all on the level," I assured her. Sky was like my mom in that she loved getting good deals, but when she could get something for nothing, well, that was cause for celebration; it made the whole day brighter. Just then, a soft knock came at the door. As I opened it, intense heat and light sliced into the dark room. Joseph stood at attention. "Here is your medicine for madam," he said.

"Thank you, Joseph," I said, handing him an American twenty-dollar bill for both the medicine and his time.

Chapter Eight

We finally found a taxi driver who claimed to know where Dr. Goodall lived. However, after a half hour of driving about aimlessly, he conceded he didn't know. Rather than get upset, Skylar asked him to take us to the U.S. Embassy, which we had passed roughly a mile back. "Yes, miss," he answered. As we pulled in front of the huge, white structure that resembled a fortress, I got all tingly when I saw the giant American flag waving proudly in the morning breeze. We entered an antechamber, and there behind bulletproof glass and thick concrete walls sat a young Marine. He was very polite but cool mannered, however once he learned Sky was from the same part of New York that he was from, he really warmed up to us. He had been a Marine for four years and had been in Dar less than one year. He was definitely homesick and asked Sky about places and people from home. Sky unfortunately didn't know anyone he knew, but I could see in his expression that this didn't matter much; the fact that she was from the same town was good enough for him. After fifteen minutes of chatter, we finally got to the point of our visit.

"Do you happen to know where Dr. Jane Goodall lives? She's a pretty famous woman who works with chimpanzees in these parts," Sky stated.

"Jane Goodall?" he repeated as he searched the depths of his memory. "I know that name sounds familiar," he added, picking up the phone to pursue our question. He spoke in mumbled tones behind the thick glass, nodded his head, and hung up.

"The woman I just spoke with, Janet, has been at this mission the longest, and she claims that Jane Goodall married some guy by the name of Bryceson. He was some big muckety-muck in the local government. He died some time back, but she still uses his last name."

"Bryceson, you said," I confirmed.

"Yeah, B-r-y-c-e-s-o-n," he spelled out, "but Janet doesn't know where she lives."

"Hey, thanks a lot," I said.

"Anything for a fellow American and person from the same town," he said, smiling at us.

"Any luck?" the driver asked as we got back into the cab.

"Do you know a Jane Bryceson?" I asked, not expecting anything. Suddenly, his eyes lit up, and he said, "Mama Bryceson! Dr. Janie! Yes, yes, I know where she lives. We will go immediately." Sky and I looked at each other as the excitement was now building. In only a few minutes, we were going to meet "Dr. Janie." Butterflies filled my stomach as the driver made a beeline for our long sought destination.

The sign on the tree read Bryceson. "Here we are, 99 Bagamoyo Road," the driver announced. We turned right onto a small dirt road and made our final approach to Dr. Goodall's residence. On my right sat a small village of homes made from mud, sticks, and tin. Clothes hung neatly from lines as warm ocean breezes gently blew them dry. A woman was sitting on a porch with her four children, who stared and pointed at the strangers driving on their road. Up ahead, nestled in among palm and pine trees and green foliage sat a large, dirty-beige home trimmed in white. It was a mansion compared with the village homes, yet it was not pretentious.

A tall young man with curly hair and a tanned face appeared at the front door. He smiled a crooked smile and welcomed us. "*Karibu*, my friends," he announced as we exited the taxi. "I'm Steve, and you must be Skylar," he said, shaking her hand.

"Pleased to meet you, Steve," she replied.

"Hi, I'm Vince," I introduced myself.

"Hey, Vince, nice to meet you," he responded, shaking my hand with a double grip. "I'm not exactly sure where Jane wants to put you, but we'll start in the guesthouse and then we can relocate you later."

"Sounds good," I responded. Steve grabbed our suitcases and carried them into a guesthouse located to the right of the main house near the water tower. It was a cozy little place with a saltwater fish tank built into a wall. The bedroom was small but comfortable and had two single beds with a mosquito net above each. Through a window, I spied the early-afternoon sun reflecting off the Indian Ocean, which was in our backyard. I called to Sky to take a look. "I love it here," she said, and wrapped her arms around me. She added, "We are so lucky."

Steve was still in the room and seemed to get a kick out of Sky's public display of affection. He asked, "Would the two of you care to join me for some afternoon tea and biscuits?"

"That sounds wonderful," Sky replied.

"Sounds great," I added.

"Well, I'll just be in the kitchen boiling some water and as soon as you're ready, come on over," he said in a pleasant tone.

Sky was still feeling a bit under the weather with a headache and decided to rest. "I'll join you in a bit. I'm going to lie down," she said.

"Okay," I replied, then kissed her. I quickly used the bathroom, washed my hands and face, and headed for the main house.

"Steve?" I called as I entered the house.

"Out here," he responded. Walking ahead, I passed through a pair of heavy double doors that opened up onto a beautiful patio constructed of decorative cement blocks. Directly ahead was a magnificent view. "Is that the Indian Ocean?" I asked.

"The Zanzibar Channel, to be precise," he said. Above us was a wooden overhang filled with beautiful green vines with blooming purple flowers, a bougainvillea. It provided natural shade as it methodically weaved its way between the gaps of the lattice overhead. Pretty much the only furniture on the patio was a set of four white wooden chairs neatly arranged around a matching table. Steve, occupying one of the chairs, looked at me. "Not bad, eh?" he asked with a grin from ear to ear.

"Not bad at all," I agreed, grabbing the teapot situated in the middle of the table and filling my cup. I sank into the cushion of my wide chair and put my feet up onto the white table, mimicking Steve. An hour passed as we got to know each other surrounded by the unparalleled beauty of nature.

Steve seemed genuinely glad to have us as guests. I mean, he was eager to show us around, and he spoke as if we were friends, despite the fact that we had just met. In fact, when I learned he had been with Jane for nearly a year, I expected he might not be into showing us the ropes. But he wasn't like that at all. No, he didn't try to extinguish the enthusiasm a newcomer feels. It was more as if he remembered how he had felt when he first arrived at Jane's and saw that soft white sand beach less than fifteen yards from where he lived, and he became excited all over again. During our conversations, he really went out of his way to make me feel at home in a place that was about as far from my home as I had ever been.

Steve was from the United States, but exactly where, I don't recall. I'm not even sure he told me. It probably had to do with the fact that he loved Africa and where he was now, so going home was the last thing on his mind. Looking around at his work environment, one knew exactly why. I recall, however, that he said Jane, as busy as she was, still found time to be a mother figure to all the young people who visited, so maybe this helped to ease any homesickness. In any case, for now, Africa was his home. In fact, he was getting ready to move to Burundi to work in a gorilla sanctuary, and he expressed his excitement over that prospect.

I liked Steve. Even though he was American, he seemed de-tached from the materialism and consumerism that occupies so much time in most Americans' lives. And Steve was using his life for a truer purpose than keeping a company in the black; he protected chimpanzees and gorillas from the greedy grasp of profiteers. I admired him, maybe even envied him a bit for standing up for something that brought him so little financial gain. I have a feeling he was much more into spiritual gain, and that made all the difference. I sat on the edge of my chair as he shared some of his experiences with me, listening intently like a son would listen to his father telling a bedtime story. What added to the magic of the moment was that he fed off my enthu-siasm, so that the more excited I got, the more into it he got. One fascinating story followed another. One bit of advice came after the next, until I felt the steady breeze on my back begin to cool, indicating the daylight was fleeing.

By the time he took a breath and I blinked, it was nearly five o'clock. "Oh, shit," Steve said abruptly. "I really need to get into town and get a few things before I pick Jane up from the airport this evening. Would you like to take a ride?"

"I think I'll stay here. I'm going to check on Sky to see how she is and get my stuff unpacked," I answered, hoping he wouldn't take it the wrong way.

"No worries, man!" he exclaimed. "I have to go into town every day, so pick a day when both of you can join me," he said.

"Sounds like a plan," I assured him.

"See you tonight," he shouted as he hurried into the house and out the front door.

I sank into the comfort of my chair and stared at the tangle of vines overhead. Then, rising from my comfort, I went to check on Sky. I peeked into the room, and there under the mosquito netting she lay soundly asleep. Quietly I closed the door in order not to wake her. I decided to take a short stroll. Walking to the water's edge, I noticed a black Labrador lying lazily in the shade of a palm. "Hey, boy," I called out. The dog raised its head briefly to see who was disturbing its rest. I noticed small patches of hair were missing all about his head and snout. "Mean fleas," I thought to myself, and he waited until I passed before resuming his prostrate position. Later I learned that he was a she named Spoof.

The beach was littered with tiny pieces of seashells, driftwood, and pine needles. A sweet smell of saltwater penetrated my nasal passage, and I recalled childhood summer trips with my family to the boardwalk in Santa Cruz. Out before me stretched a body of water that lapped repeatedly against the tiny granules of sand. I inhaled forcefully and felt the coastal air rush in and circulate through my body, and then out. "I'm finally here," I thought.

My mind was filled with questions that moment on the beach, but one thought in particular stayed with me. "What was she like?" I wondered, as anxiety grew at the thought of meeting Dr. Jane shortly. This was the woman I had often seen on *National Geographic* specials shown in class. Hell, she was known as the *National Geographic* cover girl since her fresh, pretty, young face had graced the covers of the journal frequently during the 1960s and the decades that followed, changing forever the dusty image of the magazine.

Yes, this was the same woman who had visited Dr. Louis S.B. Leakey in Kenya at the impressionable age of twenty-four. He became convinced that Jane would be an exceptional person to study the chimpanzees at Gombe. He couldn't have been more right, for her research findings would later shake the staid scientific world right down to its foundation, especially when she discovered that chimps, too, were toolmakers and users, a skill thought only to be possessed by humans. And to add insult to injury, imagine the initial reaction of the world upon hearing that such a remarkable discovery had been made by a young, female nonscientist who had just graduated from secretarial school? She didn't become Dr. Goodall until sometime later, when she wrote up her research as a doctoral dissertation at Cambridge University.

She must be quite a woman, I thought to myself, and I was about to live and work with her for a summer. This thought repeated over and over in my head.

I awoke suddenly from a short nap. Headlights could barely be seen, but the noise was unmistakable: A vehicle was coming down the road. "It's Dr. Jane!" I thought as my heart began to pump blood faster and faster to my brain. I rose from my chair and peered through a window to see a Suzuki Samurai. The door opened with a long squeak, but I saw only a head of curly light hair. I quickly concluded that it wasn't Jane or Steve, so I walked through a small, arched opening into the front driveway and introduced myself. "Hello, I'm Vince."

"Hello there, I'm Wolfgang," he answered.

"I hope you don't mind, Wolfgang, but Steve put Skylar and me up for the night in the guesthouse. Before I could get any further, he interrupted and said, "Do not worry, we have so many guests throughout the year that it is hard to keep up with who is coming and going around here. Again, welcome and I hope you have made yourselves at home." He said with a beaming smile.

"Thank you," I said. Wolfgang, like Steve, had an air of well being around him. He invited us to join him for dinner. I explained that Skylar was sleeping due to a headache and might be hungry later, but added that I was famished and would be happy to dine with him.

Wolfgang was a fisherman by profession, and if I remember correctly, he and Jane's son, Hugo, or "Grub" as he was most commonly called, were trying to get a sportfishing business going. However, they were experiencing a slight setback. "We have no boat. That's a good one, huh, a sportfishing company with no boat." He started to laugh, as did I. Apparently, they had had a boat and it was a beauty, according to Wolfgang. One day a storm moved in without warning and tore the docked boat to splinters.

"That is why Grub is not here. He is in England trying to collect insurance money to purchase a new boat. We have been sick about it ever since," he finished. In order to make ends meet, Wolfgang was now a waiter at one of the upscale hotels situated in the affluent Oyster Bay area, but he assured me that he would not be doing this long because soon Grub would return with a new boat and a fresh start toward prosperity.

As he spoke, he skillfully filleted a fish and placed it into a pan of oil, garlic, and butter. Next, he carefully sliced potatoes and placed them neatly around the fish to cook. I helped set the table as he spoke of past fishing adventures with his father. He was very animated as he spoke, asking me if I had ever been to the Amalfi Coast.

"No," I replied.

"Oh, man," he said, "that is some of the best sportfishing in the world, and it is beautiful." He stared off into space as he recalled the beauty.

As the sun ducked below the horizon, Wolfgang set three lanterns on the kitchen counter, lit them, and placed them strategically about the room. "Care for some wine?" he asked, revealing an expensive bottle of French Bordeaux. "I've been saving this for a special occasion, and this seems to be it."

"Yes, please!" I replied.

"Do you like red?" he queried.

I stood up. "I'm half Italian and half Spanish," I said. "So when I was breast-fed by my mother, it wasn't milk that came from her bosoms, one contained sangria and the other red wine!" Wolfgang chuckled at my exaggerations and I added simply, "Of course I like red." He poured me some, and we both raised our glasses for a toast. "To new friends," he said.

"To Africa," I added, and we clinked our glasses and drank down the rouge with a snort. I was no connoisseur by any means, and my enjoyment was no doubt heightened by my environment, but I'm telling you that to this day, that wine remains one of the best I have ever tasted.

The smell of fresh fish, butter, and garlic filled the air. It reminded me of my Nonna's kitchen, and this made adjusting to my new surroundings a cinch. He carefully moved the fish and potatoes around so as to not burn his fingers. He turned to me. "Another toast," he insisted and raised his glass again. He reminded me of the Ghost of Christmas Present from Charles Dickens's *A Christmas Carol* due to his zeal for life and appreciation of good food and drink. We clinked our glasses loudly for the second time, and then suddenly out of the shadows appeared Skylar. "Well, hello, miss," I said.

"Hello," she replied, rubbing her eyes. "What time is it?"

"Almost dinnertime. Are you hungry?" I asked, hoping the headache had subsided. It had, and she was feeling and looking much better. "And who is this lovely creature?" Wolfgang questioned as he reached for Sky's hand to welcome her. "Hi there, I'm Skylar," she said as her body language displayed some embarrassment for having just been asleep in a total stranger's home without proper introductions. "I'm Wolfgang and you are most welcome here and I'm glad you feel comfortable enough to take a rest." Wolfgang responded graciously, seeming to sense her slight embarrassment. "Please let's all sit; dinner is ready." And with that, we all sat and had our first dinner at 99 Bagamoyo Road.

For Skylar, serious headaches had become an accepted part of life; she had likely inherited a tendency to get them from her mother, who had suffered from full-blown migraines. Skylar's headaches were frequent and painful, but they rarely became migraines. She always carried a bottle of aspirin, popping a pill at the slightest hint of an oncoming headache. I thought this was overdoing it at first, but after nursing her through some doozies, I, too, would have popped those aspirins to reduce the chances of experiencing that kind of pain. The worst were the ones that started around her eyes and spread to other parts of her head, making her painfully sensitive to light. On occasion I sat in the dark with her, massaging her temples until the pain subsided. She told me that just as her mother had grown out of her migraines, she believed she was growing into them; the level of pain was increasing incrementally with each passing year, and she feared suffering from the same debilitating migraines as her mother.

She recalled vividly the times that her mother would become incapacitated for days due to the intense pain. "My sister and I would know when she was experiencing a migraine because her room would be dark with the curtain drawn and the door closed," Sky had explained. She and her sister would tiptoe around the house and never disturbed her unless she called. "I remember the most common question we asked my father at the breakfast table was, 'Is Mom better today?'"

The sun had set, and a hint of kerosene was in the air as we sat around the table. The lantern's glow was reflected on our faces, and the empty dishes were a testament to the delicious meal prepared by our host. We sat back with bellies full, and our conversation darted from one topic to the next, from one end of the spectrum to the other. We talked until our throats grew scratchy, then we talked some more. No television, no radio, no electric lights. Just us, the kerosene lamps, and our imaginations were all we needed to keep the conversation moving and interesting. Each of us searched the caverns of our memory to recall past stories, anecdotes, and facts to share with the others.

Suddenly the sound of an engine grew close and headlights shone bright on the walls through the screen door. It was Steve returning from the airport with Dr. Jane. A nervous excitement grew as butterflies filled my stomach. I picked up my wine glass and sipped down its contents to calm myself, but my skin wanted to jump from my bones as I awaited her entrance for what seemed like an eternity. Then we heard, "Hello there," as a soft voice called in through the screen door.

"Hello, Jane, come on in. Would you care for a glass of wine?" Wolfgang offered.

"That would be wonderful," she answered politely, standing before me. Skylar quickly rose to her feet to greet Dr. Goodall. "Nice to see you again, Skylar," Jane said. She seemed genuinely glad to see her. They had gotten to know one another while Jane was visiting the College of William and Mary, so Sky was in a different boat than I was. She was cool and collected. I, on the other hand, was a bundle of nerves.

Then the moment of truth: Sky turned to me, and her mouth moved in slow motion as she formed the words "And this is Vince, the journalist from California." I swallowed hard, stood, and told Dr. Goodall I admired her work and was honored to finally meet her. I sat back down without a flubbed word. Amazingly, it appeared as if she blushed slightly at my compliments. Imagine that, a woman who has met presidents and dined with royalty, but still blushed at being complimented. I found that not only refreshing, but very human and reassuring.

Wolfgang had given Jane his seat. He crouched next to her, and they discussed the house and monthly bills as she switched from chimp savior Jane to domestic Jane.

Having just returned from a month-long trip that took her to the U.K. and North America and back through East Africa, she was tired. She looked gaunt, and her arm faltered slightly as she lifted her wine glass to her lips. But instead of retreating to bed, she stayed up with us, joining the conversation and explaining with a youthful glimmer in her eyes the projects Skylar and I could help her with. However, she lost me when she mentioned we would be traveling to Kigoma for an exhibition of Jane Goodall Institute projects for the local schoolchildren. At times reality seemed overwhelming. Here I was, sitting next to one of the premier primatologists in the world, and I would be living, eating, and traveling with her for four weeks. Not bad for a guy who thought his world had ended when he learned he didn't get into Harvard Law School. Instead, another door to the world had opened.

The lanterns began to sputter, their glass blackened by smoke, as the five of us started yawning and stretching one by one. The moon was full and the clouds that surrounded it caused a celestial glow. The light on the water's surface was white and shimmered as gentle currents made themselves known. When conversations about politics and religion seem to mirror the world's ugliness, one can always look to nature to counterbalance that and mirror the world's splendor. So for a moment, the five of us forgot the troubles of the world and reflected upon how beautiful it could be at times. Finally, Jane softly said, "Well good night. I'm off to bed."

Chapter Nine

The next morning, the house was abuzz with activity. It was nearly nine o'clock, and Jane had already been up for hours, writing, preparing, thinking, and so on. Entering the kitchen, I noticed an electric kettle bringing water to a boil. French bread had been sliced and toasted, and next to it stood a jar of preserves brought from England. "Help yourself," Steve said.

As I bit into a piece of toast, its tiny air pockets crunched, releasing melted butter and preserves into my mouth and triggering immediate satisfaction. I walked through the heavy double doors into the fresh morning air, the kind that a fisherman would experience every morning. The sun shimmered on the water, illuminating different shades of green and blue, and small whitecaps dotted the surface. Small waves collapsed along the shore, and white seagulls gracefully skimmed the water's surface for a morning meal. Over to my right lay another dog. This one, too, lifted its head slightly to see who was wandering about. It had beautifully striped short hair, and it rested comfortably on a soiled white cushion. This was Saranda, I later learned. Her eyes closed in satisfaction as I knelt down to pet her. An outburst of interesting birdcalls sounded from one treetop to the next, blending with the faint sound of motorboats cutting across the Zanzibar Channel. All of this, held in light so clear and focused, looked like a photo that had been airbrushed or otherwise retouched.

I was curious to see the rest of the house, so I went on a

self-guided tour of downstairs. Walking back through the heavy doors, I saw a bright sitting room on my right. Three of its four walls were constructed entirely of glass, with windows you could open to let in the sweet aroma of the sea. The ceiling, door, and one wall were painted a crisp white. Five chairs, similar to the patio set, were the centerpieces of the room, ringing a glass coffee table. In the corner stood a table with a stack of reading material that ranged from pamphlets written in Swahili to copies of *Time* and *National Geographic*. In another corner stood a table with a lamp, another stack of reading material, and a chair. This was where Jane would do some of her writing. The ceiling fan blades turned slowly and circulated ocean air about the room. A lone bookshelf sat against the one wall that was not glass and was filled with paperback and hardcover books. By the end of our stay, this room had become my favorite because it was here that we gathered most. It had the most favorable climate of any room in the house, and it was where countless storytelling sessions took place, but I will get to that later.

The kitchen could be seen through a small serving window and sat directly behind the solid wall of the sitting room. Like Jane, it was simple and had all that was essential. Its light blue countertops were cluttered with packages of food, and the tiny electric stove looked as if it received plenty of use. A small refrigerator sat alone against the far wall and was mostly filled with soft drinks and beer for company. A steel sink basin looked onto the front yard of the house and was an ideal spot to observe approaching visitors. Dishes seemed to be in a constant process of either being dirtied or drying on the rack, but rarely were they put away, mainly due to the steady stream of guests.

In the foyer, there was a desk with a comfortable armchair. A telephone sat atop it, along with a pen and a blank pad of paper. I could tell that whoever used this pad last was a hard writer, for the top page had clear, legible impressions that read, "Pick Jane up at six thirty from the airport! Don't be late!"

Against a wall directly facing the front door was an antique table with two leaves folded down. It caught my eye because atop it, next to a beautiful, handmade fluted basket, sat a toy chimpanzee. "This must be Jubilee," I said to myself. Jubilee was part of a limited edition that honored the birth of a baby chimpanzee on the same day as the Silver Jubilee of King George V and Queen Mary. Due to the timing of the birth of the baby chimp, the toy was appropriately named Jubilee. The story goes that one of these toy chimpanzees was given to Jane when she was two or three years old and became the impetus for her lifelong fascination with and commitment to these animals. Some years later, after reading books about Dr. Doolittle, she coupled this early love for chimps with the hope of someday living in Africa, and the rest, as the saying goes, is history.

Personally, I find these stories cute and interesting for children, but it takes much more than a toy and a book to inspire the longest field study of animals in history. I often wonder at the level of personal commitment Jane maintains year after year, and the unwavering focus on wildlife, especially her chimpanzees. It would be nice if all this could be initiated by early-childhood toys and storybooks, but it was something deep within her psyche that led Jane to Africa. And what about the energy it takes to keep that fire stoked, to keep her passion burning just as clean and bright in her later years as it did on the day she first landed in Gombe! Yes, the more I learned about this woman, the more in awe of her I became.

Walking upstairs, I saw Jane sitting at the desk in her study and reading aloud to herself. "Please, please, please, don't throw away my letter. Please help me. Help, help me," she was saying. As I stood at the doorway to her study to listen to her, she stopped reading and turned to me. "Hi there," she said.

"Good morning," I replied. She then went right back to the letter. "This young girl from Romania has written me and wants to come to Africa," she told me with a troubled look on her face.

"Oh, dear," she said, shaking her head and placing the letter onto a pile of letters she would answer. One of Jane's many hallmarks was that no matter how busy she was, she always made time to personally respond to letters. Jane was one of those people who really cared, and this was what I would come to truly treasure.

Jane grabbed another letter and began to read aloud again as I looked around the study. A dark wooden bookcase, nine shelves high, reached from floor to ceiling. It bulged with material in colored bindings and painted aeclectic picture. The only uniform color was the yellow that ran across the top shelf, the spines of many years of *National Geographic*.

The desk where Jane sat was overflowing with paper, and I wondered how she was able to find anything. Another, much smaller desk faced Jane's and was buttressed against it. This was covered less thoroughly with papers but was cluttered nonetheless. She caught me staring at the chaotic desktops and announced, "There is a method to my madness, I assure you, Vince!" She smiled quickly and went back to reading.

The walls of the study were a cool green-blue and had a relaxing effect. Two metal file cabinets rested side by side with a hand-painted picture set on top, leaning against the cool wall and awaiting a nail. In the corner was a photograph of a chimpanzee sitting patiently next to a mound of termites. In his hand was a wide blade of grass that he had purposely sheared so he could carefully dip it into the mound's entrance in order to extract the tasty contents. This was David Graybeard and as soon as Jane observed and wrote about his actions, this previously unknown ability to use tools would amaze the scientific community, changing forever the way the world viewed the evolution of the human race.

Skylar was busy on the beach searching for sticks and twigs so that she could make replicas of chimp tools for the exhibit in Kigoma. She sat, patiently studying the pictures Jane had given her. When she saw me approaching, she looked relieved and asked, "Do you want to help?"

"Yeah, sure," I replied. And so we sat in the shade of a cluster of palm trees, fashioning chimp tools for half the day. We spoke of all the wonderful things we had seen and shared in the nearly two weeks we had been in Africa. It was amazing how well the two of us traveled together. She was definitely the better-prepared traveler, since she always had a snack or drink handy to ease our hunger or quench our thirst. I was definitely the more adventurous, always seeking out different hikes we could take in the surrounding terrain. She, a willing partner, was ready to venture into any situation.

The coming weeks in Africa would witness our growing together as a serious couple. We shared moments of intimacy that I never thought possible between two people, and she restored my faith in the idea that for every person there is an ideal match or soul mate. She brought out the best in me, the man I wanted to be, and I loved her for it, and I only hoped I did the same for her. One night as we lay in bed side by side, staring into the darkness, surrounded only by the soft material of the mosquito net and air, she turned to me and said, just above a whisper, "Vince, you make me feel whole." I knew at that moment that the emotional stakes had increased tenfold and left both of us vulnerable, for in only three weeks we would return to our respective worlds. The challenge that lay before us was to bridge those two worlds without stifling personal growth or jeopardizing the plans we had committed to before we met. Although I didn't agonize over this reality, it became the first thing I thought about upon rising each morning, along with a plummeting feeling in the pit of my stomach.

That evening was the chilliest in Dar upon Jane's recollection. We had just finished *another* meal of toasted French bread topped with cheese and fresh tomatoes. Outside of that first meal with Wolfgang, all of our meals with Dr. Jane were simple and provided enough nutrients to keep us going and made maintaining ones weight for rigorous travel quite easy. I learned through Jane that it didn't take a whole lot of food to keep a person running efficiently. Everyone in the house at that time , except me, was a vegetarian so all our meals were limited to cheese, milk, eggs, grains, fruits, and vegetables. Pasta with tomato sauce, rice, fried eggs on toast, and grilled cheese with tomato on French bread served as lunches and dinners, while cereal and fruit were our breakfast staples. This simple repertoire continued for nearly four weeks until I returned to the tasty pollutants of home and convenience. I personally found my diet, while in Africa, resulted in large amounts of energy, clearer thinking, and a more even temperament. Moreover, when I saw how meat was handled at the local markets, my craving for animal flesh subsided. Let's just say it wasn't the neat little packages wrapped in cellophane we pick up at Safeway. American meat is handled in the same brutal fashion as meat in Africa, but in America this is usually not visible to the consumer, which makes eating meat much easier.

Steve rose and thoughtfully collected the dinner dishes from the small table. "Shall I bring out the bottle of Scotch and four glasses?" Steve asked with delight.

"Yes, that sounds good," Jane replied, "but let's retire to the sitting room. What do you think?" She looked at Skylar, who had managed to tuck her legs under her sweatshirt so that it looked like a small tent covering her body.

"If nobody else minds," she replied, looking at me.

"Let's go," I said, springing to my feet. Steve was busy in the kitchen gathering four glasses and a bottle of single-malt Scotch. I had never drunk Scotch before, not to mention single-malt. He brought out a tray bearing four short glasses filled halfway with the expensive and hard-to-acquire liquid. "Here you are," he said as he handed over each glass. He bent and set the tray at his feet, then straightened up and toasted Skylar and me, adding that he was happy we were there. Skylar then returned the honor and raised her glass. "To our gracious hosts," she said, "and ensuring that we may always remember this summer."

"Here, here," we all agreed, and then I took a sip. The liquid slipped between my lips, over my teeth, and onto my tongue. It stung at first touch, and my taste buds jumped to life. The vapors from the liquid caused my nasal passages to open wide as it rolled over my tongue, sending all sorts of impulses throughout my mouth, then down my throat it went. I felt it travel every inch of my esophagus and drop into my gut—all of this within a second or two. The intoxicating liquid helped to relax the atmosphere, and soon the room was alive with conversation.

Jane began to describe the financial troubles that the Jane Goodall Institute was experiencing. This came as a shock, especially when she announced that unless certain things changed, "the whole program will come to a grinding halt in only a few months' time."

"What can be done to avert that?" I asked.

"Well, we are obviously doing everything we can at the moment, but one factor of crucial importance is that we get a new director. There is one gentleman, Don Buford, that I feel will do an exceptional job." Mr. Buford was a Texan and a successful political consultant. He was also a whiz at fund-raising, a talent that was desperately needed at the almost-destitute institution. Jane had met with Don a few times, but it wasn't clear whether he was going to accept the job or not. Even if he did, that still didn't guarantee the institute could be saved.

Despite this crisis, Jane managed to keep up a grueling schedule and even took on extra work as a result of the crisis. However, not once during our conversation did she express despair or utter that common phrase used often during times of trouble, "Why me? " She just explained the situation and how she intended to fix it. That's it. I would probably have audibly mourned the years of research and hours spent championing chimpanzees. As it was, I worried a great deal that what took nearly four decades of work to develop might come crashing down in a few short months.

Not Jane, though. She was tempered like a fine piece of steel. And we would learn of her tempering as the night wore on and she recalled living through the war.

"I was a young schoolgirl, when Britain's air space was invaded by Nazi warplanes. Hitler had brought Western Europe to its knees, and his plan of total domination included conquering the U.K. Undefeated and assuming an air of invincibility, Germany considered Britain as an obstacle rather than a legitimate threat to the Reich."

She continued to tell us that her father had enlisted and many of their family friends had been killed. Around 1940, the Battle of Britain raged and London and surrounding towns were pounded mercilessly. Jane told us that every night they had to blackout their windows and on occasion bombs would drop in surrounding areas where she lived causing thunderous explosions, as German aircraft made their way back to Germany. When the war ended and Europe was rebuilding, it was the images of the destruction caused by war and the Holocaust that continued to have a profound effect on her. "I remember seeing images in the newspapers of the once beautiful cities throughout Europe now reduced to rubble and the stacked bodies, mostly skeletons, of what were once people and thought how could this happen?" She closed her eyes and shook her head. Her expression was as if she was still feeling the shock of these horrible images of war from her childhood.

I remember once overhearing a conversation my grandfather was having with a man who had lived through the bombings of Britain. He commented, "After the war was over, it was like you were reborn. As if all those things that were once difficult were now a little easier, and your troubles didn't seem to affect you as much because you always recalled those times in the shelter and hearing the explosions. I guess the experience, as dreadful as it was, helped to make my life a little easier later on, and from there on out, I always placed things within the context of war. Nothing seemed to shake me up as much after the war. I just dealt with it." Although Jane never said anything to that effect, I believe she would have shared this man's sentiments. Perhaps this explains why her determination knew no bounds and why her aspirations seemed to have no limits.

The conversation abruptly went from her experiences as a child during the Second World War to the malfunctioning state of the walkie-talkies at Gombe. Jane was contemplating out loud how to bring new radios into Tanzania rather than buying them locally, where the price was triple what one could buy them for in the U.K. or the States. I got the impression that with the growing winds of a possible financial disaster on the heels of every project funded by the Jane Goodall Institute, certain essentials could not be purchased as they had been before. Instead, donations or gifts would be necessary to acquire the essential items like radios, so researchers could communicate over the thirty square miles at Gombe. Jane wasn't being disingenuous. No, that wasn't her style. She only wanted to bend the rules, not break them.

"Can you have people who come to visit bring radios with them?" I inquired. "I mean, if you had asked Skylar and me, we could have brought a few."

"Yes, but if it is over a certain number, you must pay a heavy tax, and that doesn't make it worth the effort. No, there must be a better way," she said with the mischievous look of a school-child.

A silence descended over the room for the first time in three hours. Steve stood and stretched. "I think I'm ready for bed," he announced with a small yawn. Goodnights were said all around, and Steve left the room. Soon after, Skylar excused herself, and then there were two. I looked at Jane; she stared silently out the glass walls into the darkness.

As I cleared my throat, the sound brought her out of her trance and back to the room. "Where were you?" I asked.

"Oh, just contemplating all of the things that must be done. That's all," she answered in a low voice.

"Jane," I asked, "do you ever get lonely?"

"That's a silly question!" she exclaimed, slightly perplexed. "Of course I do. Everyone gets lonely at times." I was well aware of that, but Jane, on occasion, seemed to carry an air of loneliness even when besieged by a room full of friends and devotees. At times a similar contradiction seemed to descend upon the beach-front house. At the very times when the old house was filled with visitors and all sorts of activity, a powerful sensation of weariness was present within the concrete walls. I wanted to share my thoughts with Jane, but I wasn't sure if I genuinely felt this or if it was the Scotch talking, so I decided to play it safe and wished Jane a good night.

"Good night, sleep well," she acknowledged.

Chapter Ten

The next day, Skylar and I moved into the upstairs bedroom in the big house. Jane was expecting other guests
and decided we would be much more comfortable in this
room. She was right. It was about three times the size of my
room back home and had a double bed and French doors that
opened onto a balcony with a panoramic view of the channel. A
pleasant smell of rainwater and soap rose as Skylar unfolded
freshly washed sheets to put on the bed. When she finished, she
carefully placed a picture of her mother and father next to her
side of the bed, while I set up my laptop computer and printer
on the large desk and wished I had brought a photo of my
family.

The sun shone beautifully into the walled space, and with the
exception of the channel view, the windows were by far my favorite feature of the room. The light provided inspiration and
helped to stir creative juices that enabled me to assist Jane in
writing letters, posing ideas, and most important, helping to develop and expand Roots and Shoots.

Roots and Shoots was an international youth program started
by Jane to encourage young people to get involved in various
causes through activities that focused on three central themes:
community, environment, and animal welfare. Jane glowed with
pride as she described how R&S groups in countries all over the
world had been writing to tell her of all the work they had been
doing for their communities. "They've started recycling programs, organized weekly litter collection days and tree planting

parties, and raised funds for chimpanzees and other endangered animals through bake sales. I tell you, it gives these young citizens such pride and purpose to know that they are part of something bigger than themselves," she stated with conviction.

Hell, being part of something bigger than me was why I had begun to write about youth issues, and it was what had ultimately led me to Jane. I clearly understood how important it is to pass this sense of purpose on to others. And so with limited resources, enthusiasm, and the sun dancing happily on the walls, Sky and I began to do what we could for the expansion of Roots and Shoots. Of immediate concern was the development of an information sheet that could be passed easily from hand to hand, student to student, explaining in detail exactly what R&S was and how a group could start their own Roots and Shoots club. Jane thought a pamphlet might be nice, but due to the constraints on funds, this seemed to be out of the question. Pressed to perform other tasks, Jane announced confidently, "I will leave you two to your own devices and see what you can come up with."

Skylar and I tossed around ideas for a few hours. "How about this?" I would say.

"Too expensive," she would reply. "What if we did this?"

Then we would both respond in sync, "No," shaking our heads and laughing.

Trying out ideas continued until we returned to Jane's original idea of creating a pamphlet. We both believed this would be the best format because it would serve two important ends. First, it would be informative, and second, it would give the impression of a well-organized group, one that children and young people would be proud to belong to. Creating an informative and nice-looking pamphlet would attract attention and result in new membership. So this was our first decision: We agreed that a pamphlet would be the vehicle to spread the word of this movement. Now we had to decide what information to include and how to keep costs at a minimum. Skylar focused on the former, and I, the latter.

After wrestling with various possibilities, I finally came up with something that seemed like it would work. I gathered the images and words from various documents Jane had scattered around her office. We had agreed earlier what would appear on the cover, so I cut out the images and words and carefully pasted them on a sheet of white paper. I then did the same with the images and words that would appear on the back. I folded the paper exactly in half and it formed the perfect exterior for our pamphlet. While it was a very elementary accomplishment, I was proud of it because it was created with limited resources. Skylar had made similar gains. She quickly decided that the pamphlet would consist of seven points of information: Our Philosophy, Taking Action, What You Can Do, Funding, Starting A Club, Existing Clubs, and Membership Information. I sat at the computer and she paced behind me as we both searched our creative wells for the proper words. Through our joint efforts, it didn't take long for each section to come to life. We brought Jane the rough draft. As she stared at it in silence, we awaited her approval.

Looking up at us, a broad smile came to her face. "I think this just might work!" she exclaimed. "Put it all together tomorrow and let's have a look at the finished piece," she added in a reserved but good-natured manner.

It was nearly five o'clock, and we continued working in an effort to finish our project. But when the electricity went out, crippling our ability to use the printer and copier, it became evident that we would have to finish it the next day.

That evening at dinner, we were hungrier than in previous evenings, for we had gone without lunch. Afterward, we sat in the glass room and talked until sleepiness finally caught up with us. We were in heightened spirits as a result of the successful labor on the pamphlet. In addition to our project, we had taken on extra tasks, such as letter writing and searching the study for documents that Jane knew were somewhere in the study but wasn't quite sure about the exact drawer, shelf, box, or closet— although, I must say, she was well organized and had already proved to me that there truly was a method to her mess.

As we retired to bed, Steve called out from the kitchen, "Hey, guys, I'm going into the city tomorrow. Would you like to join me?"

"Yeah! Sure!" we replied one after the other.

"All right then, tomorrow about ten o'clock," Steve confirmed.

"Fine," Skylar answered, and we continued our ascent up the stone steps to our room.

That evening was still. Not a gust of wind blew, nor a branch trembled. Not even the smallest leaf shook that night. Skylar lay in silence, not quite asleep, as she nursed the final minutes of a brutal headache that had suddenly snuck up on her after dinner. I took solace in an armchair that I had placed squarely in the open doorway. A candle warmly glowed, filling the room with a light dim enough to allow sleep, but bright enough to read by. I periodically lifted my eyes from my book to catch a glimpse of the placid waters reflected in the moonlight that seemed to fill the silence. Behind me, Skylar, thoroughly exhausted from wrestling with the pain from her headache, had slipped from consciousness into a deep, relaxing sleep that was revealed by her deep slow breaths.

The wax slowly dripped down to the candle's base and met the rest of the wax that had fallen. I set the book open over my knee as I yawned and took a long stretch. The air remained still, but the silence had given way to a rising sound that carried to my ears from the small village of houses located in the belt of trees to the front of the big house. The sound was music, and the music expressed a happiness that seemed foreign to a man from the West. It was the type of happiness that could be found only in family and spiritual enlightenment. It seemed to be the credo of the people of that small village nestled in the trees. Even though I had never heard it as clearly as I did that motionless evening, it was the one thing that occurred with clockwork consistency during all my nights in Dar.

Skylar and I came to call the villagers the common people. These folks served as the backbone of the larger community; they had the lean muscles and fiery characters that seemed to propel societies forward, although they were largely unnoticed and unrewarded. There, half hidden among the trees, they happily dwelled. I peeked out the small window that overlooked the area from which the sound rose. The music had faded from the forefront to a steady backdrop. Now it was the voices of these people that found their way into my ears, the voices of individuals who toiled tirelessly each day and then delighted each evening with song, fire, food, and drink. I watched as the incandescent light from their fires cast large shadows undulating against the belt of trees as if they were spirits caught in a struggle between the world here and the afterlife. Suddenly the candle that had burned so steadily in the room flickered for a long moment, as if struggling to stay alight, but finally fell black, as if signaling me that it was time for bed. I quietly got into bed and settled comfortably under the cool sheets. The stillness of the evening air had passed, but celebration persisted and helped me to sleep.

Recurring quips and phrases awakened me to an early-morning fog, a gray barrier between the earth and the sun's warming rays. "Jane is in the study," I thought to myself. I knew she was there because she was thinking aloud again as she read more letters.

The thought of finishing the pamphlet caused me to rise, although I was still craving a few more hours of sleep. I dressed and went to the kitchen to find a fresh pot of French pressed coffee. I poured myself a cup, and then slowly walked back upstairs sipping and enjoying the warm aromatic brew. "Good morning, Jane," I said, passing the open door to the study heading to the room with the copier.

"Up already?" Jane asked.

"Yeah, I couldn't sleep anymore," I answered. The rough draft of the pamphlet cover and its contents sat atop the copy machine. A green light blinked, indicating the copier was ready to go. The power had returned. I picked up the papers and brought them to my room. I sat at the large desk and began to carefully cut out each section and paste it on the reverse side of the cover. Skylar awoke when she heard me cursing the pamphlet and my inability to cut a straight line at six in the morning. Ten minutes later she was sitting beside me, cutting and pasting.

We stared at the finished rough draft. It looked more like a paper Frankenstein than a professional pamphlet, but Skylar assured me that once she brushed over all the seams with whiteout and produced multiple copies, it would look whole. I approached the copier with apprehension, for this was the moment of truth. I could tell by Sky's expression that even she hoped her words would ring true about the pamphlet looking whole and professional once reproduced. I asked Sky to do the honors. "Thanks," she said in a sarcastic tone. She carefully placed the cover in the indicated space, lowered the copier's lid, and pressed the glowing green button. A rumbling sound was heard from the rectangular box as it performed its duty. A flash occurred and a piece of paper appeared from the side. Back home you would expect a clean fresh copy but here you maybe had a 50/50 chance of success. I grabbed it and we both examined it in silence under the light. Our sense of excitement grew as we carefully placed that copy back into the paper tray so the next copy would appear on the reverse side of the clean-copied cover. Again we placed the paper to be copied carefully on the glass and lowered the top. A rumble, a flash, and then the piece of paper appeared from the side once more. It was crisp and clean with only a few lines of black, but that was okay. I carefully folded the paper exactly in half, and now in my hands was a pamphlet. We examined the cover, lifted the fold, and inside, we found the different sections of information we wrote looking us squarely in the face. We closed the fold to examine the back cover. We giggled with excitement over the completion of our project. It wasn't that what we had done was a masterpiece, for in reality, it was quite simple. Our elation came from the knowledge that we had wanted to create a pamphlet, and through sheer will, and using only the material at hand, we brought this idea from the recesses of our minds to the children of Dar. I know this sounds hugely, almost comically inflated in terms of our excitement over the creation of a two sided flyer, however you need to understand that we were in a city where things did not work on a regular basis. If something broke down it more than likely remained broken for a long period of time because it was so expensive to find and purchase replacement parts. Additionally, power could go out for long stretches of time making the completion of a simple project drag on indefinitely. So to complete this pamphlet in a timely manner so that we could use them today as opposed to weeks, maybe a month from now was something to celebrate. We brought the finished product to Jane and our excitement became hers. She was thrilled that the electricity was back and the copier was functioning. She looked at it quickly and made a few changes, but it remained largely intact. Passing it back to Skylar she said, "Quickly my dear, make those changes and let's get 500 copies done before our luck with the copier runs out!"

With the changes made we began to make the copies that would end up in the hands of hundreds of school children in Dar. Watching the machine spit out these pamphlets brought us great satisfaction. We were proud not only of the completed work but the message within. That message read as follows:

"Roots and Shoots emphasizes the value of each individual, whether human or nonhuman. We believe every individual has a part to play. Every individual can make a difference. This leads to respect for all life. Members should strive to give young people a better understanding of both animal and human nature and the many problems that human greed has inflicted upon the environment. Armed only with compassion and love, knowledge and understanding, persistence and hard work, the youth of a community can help heal the world." The simple message that Skylar and I struggled to pen that summer day still causes my chest to swell with pride upon each reading.

Suddenly a horn sounded as Steve sat in the Rover, eager to leave for the city. Skylar and I rushed about, carefully folding the pamphlets and stacking them in a box. Jane had come in earlier and informed us that we should begin to disseminate the pamphlets as soon as possible. So we planned to make short presentations and pass out the pamphlets at several local primary schools in Dar over the next few days, beginning that very afternoon, until we left for Kigoma. Nervous because we wanted everything to be perfect, we both secretly wished that we hadn't agreed to visit the city with Steve that day so we could work on our presentation. However, he was so excited to show us around Dar that neither of us had the heart to tell him, so off to the city we went.

As we journeyed to the city, what I saw before me resembled what I might have seen in the Old West of the United States more than a century ago. The uneven dirt road was wide, with rows of buildings on either side that stretched for miles. Instead of horses strapped to hitching posts, there were beat-up trucks and cars, mostly Fords and Toyotas, sprinkled along the main street. "Is this the main market?" I asked Steve.

"No, this is a small village market," he replied. "Each village has its own." Despite its small size, energy coursed through the street. This was the village's heart, and the people in the streets were the precious blood that kept it pumping. Together they helped each other thrive. This was where the people came to buy goods for their homes, medical supplies for their children, food for their bellies, and shoes for their feet.

On either side of this main road, buildings were placed one next to the other, creating a patchwork effect. Rickety, sixty-year-old wooden structures with rusty tin roofs, broken porches, and cracked windows stood shoulder to shoulder with a newer brick structure that had a beautiful tile roof and thick cement porch. The contrast was blatant, and the look disjointed, but it worked. I thought these buildings also served as a sort of timeline. For example, in one building you might have woven goods for sale. These goods were usually crafted by hand through methods handed down generation after generation. The building next to it might be the pharmacy, for example, which indicated the introduction of newer ways brought to Africa by various religious missions and imperial colonizers.

We continued to drive as the facades of village buildings slipped by and the rich foliage returned to the roadside. We passed a vendor who had nestled his handcrafted furniture under the shade of several trees. Displayed on the shady patches of dirt was months of this man's work. Everything (chairs, tables, rugs, and stools) was meticulously arranged, and the man stood by the roadside, eagerly awaiting customers. Then the trees and foliage gave way once again to man-made structures, but this time they were huge houses with high cement walls and gates. "The wealthy," I thought. Vines desperately clung to unnatural barriers in an effort to reclaim former territory, but it was a losing effort; they just hung like possessions on the fortress walls. Then the houses were gone, and miles of white beaches started.

As the soft, white sand jutted out to meet the blue water, clouds moved in and were scattered about. Some even appeared to be sitting on the water's surface. This helped to protect us from the sun's glare, but the humidity was stifling. I had showered only an hour earlier, and I was due for another. I turned to look at Sky, who was wiping away sweat as it rolled down and stung her cheeks. I smiled and she did too. The silence was victorious for now but would soon be broken by chaotic happenings inside the capital city.

In 1850, Dar es Salaam was a sleepy fishing village. Some fifty years later, it had grown to become the capital of Tanzania. This transformation was primarily due to the harbor's suitability for large steam vessels, which led to a flourishing trade market. Today, modern Dar boasts a population of nearly a million and a half. And while it is obvious that things have changed dramatically since Dar's humble beginnings, there are things that haven't changed at all. I found that the majority of Dar's colonial attributes were still intact. As the harbor slowly established itself in our view, I noticed untouched rows of palms and mangroves still skirting the harbor as they had for more than a hundred years. Modern fishing vessels with their state-of-the-art radar and offshore communications systems bobbed in the harbor as they mingled with dugout canoes. Although unsophisticated, the dugout was a highly effective original fishing vessel of these waters. And roped to the Malindi docks were Arab dhows, which still ferried people from Dar to Zanzibar and back, just as they had done at the end of the last century. Directly behind these preserved images sat three buildings made of cement, glass, and steel that stretched up toward the clouds. These were some of the high-rises that increasingly punctuated the city center. However, Dar remains primarily a city of low-rise buildings with distinctive, red-tiled roofs.

Continuing along the water, I noticed a collection of small kiosks constructed from old Pepsi billboards with names including "The Beach Kiosk" and "Original Kiosk." Each kiosk carried the same thing: hot samosas and cases of Coca-Cola. I thought of the article I had just read that attributed malnutrition to the consumption of Coke in developing countries. Let's face it, almost every kid I knew loved Coke, at least every kid in my neighborhood, and the children of Africa were no different. What was different, however, was the price. In a developing country, the purchase of soft drinks like Coke usually compromised the ability to purchase more nutritious staples like bread or milk. In fact, this scenario is so prevalent that nutrition experts had named it the Coke Syndrome. Here before me stood a row of these soft drink vendors and people with young children queuing for a bottle or two. I wondered if the parents knew about this study. How many of these children would suffer from malnutrition because their parents just wanted to treat them to a Coke?

● ● ●

Pulling into the heart of the city, we parked, and Steve told us he would be in the KLM office arranging for Jane's flight to Canada. "Feel free to walk about, but stay close because we need to get back to the house by two this afternoon."

"No problem. I'm going to just snoop around for a bit," I said, lacing up my boots. Sky stretched and let out a yawn and slowly got out. I stepped from the Land Rover onto a shard of glass that crunched under my boot.

The streets were narrow and packed with cars. People walked the busy sidewalks, going about their daily tasks. I immediately noticed how well preserved the concrete buildings of colonial heritage were, and how the disparities between the poorer sections and wealthier sections weren't as flagrant as they were in most crowded, large African capitals. In fact, I would definitely liken Dar to a capital city in Western Europe for two reasons: first, its European layout and architecture, characterized by narrow streets with tall, columned buildings on either side, numerous iron-railed balconies, and windows that opened to the busy streets below; and second, its fashion. I found the people in Dar were a particularly well-dressed group. Many of the businessmen wore stylish suits and ties, while business-women wore stylish dresses. But beyond that, even regular Dar-ians on an outing to the city sported collared shirts, slacks, and dresses.

As I continued to walk, cool ocean breezes blew in and up the narrow streets, removing the carbon monoxide spewing from autos in the congested passages. People smiled and laughed and embraced openly. Bicyclists darted between cars as they went about delivering messages held securely in their baskets. What I saw before me was a far cry from the images I had grown accustomed to on late-night television, those depict-ing an appalling disparity between the haves and the have-nots, portraying Africans as barefoot and wrapped in ragged clothes with outstretched hands in need of assistance. Hell, I'd been con-vinced *that* was Africa! It was tantamount to seeing nothing but images of the violent crimes that happen every day in America and saying, "This is America." If countries were considered to have character, like individuals do, the people responsible for those broadcast images would be guilty of character assassina-tion and should be ashamed of themselves. I can confidently say that what I saw in Dar, was a vibrant city steeped in culture, dig-nity, and growing prosperity—like the other parts of East Africa I visited—not the misleading nonsense used in TV spots to raise money.

I returned after a half hour had passed, and waiting in the Rover were Steve and Sky. "How was your look around?" Steve queried.

"In a word, enlightening," I replied seriously.

Steve nodded. "Right on, man," he encouraged me in his laid-back tone.

The drive back was long because the road was clogged and traffic slowed to a grinding halt near the first village market we had seen. Villagers walked the streets, gathered on corners, and sat on the benches that occupied many of the older wooden porches. They stared into our vehicle, plugging along slowly next to the halted procession of cars. All of a sudden, I became uncomfortably conscious of the fact that I was white. I had been in Africa for just shy of a month, and it was the first time I felt different because I was not black. It really made me insecure. I wondered what they saw when they stared at me. Did they see a man, or did they see the epitome of all that was wrong with Africa? I wondered what emotions they felt toward me. Was it hatred for the color of my skin? I mean, if I had bad manners or the wrong clothes on, I could change that, but if it was the pigment of my skin, well, there was nothing I could do. There was no way of hiding that. Nothing could be bought to conceal that. What a feeling to be ashamed of your own color, I thought. This feeling caused me to reflect upon the sad fact that some people in America hated people just because of their dark skin. For them, skin color signified a deviant, a criminal, somebody different, a minority. And while all these assumptions are false, some people adhere to them nonetheless. This theme of color and prejudice would trail me like a private detective for the rest of the day.

Back at Jane's, I changed my clothes and put on a dress shirt and a pair of slacks. I knew it was just a primary school we'd be visiting, but I really wanted to make a good impression. Besides, it had become apparent to me that many white visitors seemed to think that just because they were in Africa they could get away with grungy clothes. It was as if, all of a sudden, standards of appearance had dropped. This especially typified younger visitors, who often thought that personal hygiene and nice clothes stopped existing in Africa. I thought this an ignorant brand of stereotyping because if one paused to take a serious look around, most Africans were dressed well and were neat in appearance, especially in the cities. Of the people I saw, none were in ripped or badly frayed clothes. Even if they were poor, it was my observation that they took great pride in their appearance. So out of respect, I dressed as I would if attending any school presentation. I wanted to look neat and professional.

I grabbed dozens of pamphlets and met Jane and Skylar in the Land Rover. They, too, were well dressed, and I could sense that Jane was pleased at our efforts to make a good impression.

Arriving, we found that the school grounds were empty, for the school day had ended. However, gathered in a classroom and patiently waiting for us was a large group of primary students. As we entered, conversations suddenly went silent as all the attention was focused on us. A teacher rose from behind her desk, *"Karibu,* Dr. Jane," she said in greeting. Jane and the tall, slender teacher spoke in a mixture of Swahili and English. Skylar and I felt curious stares penetrating us as we walked through the neat rows of desks passing out our freshly printed flyers to eagerly awaiting hands. Finished we returned to the head of the class. *"Karibu,"* the teacher said to me and Skylar, shaking our hands. "It is a pleasure to have you join us."

We were seated at the front of the class as Jane began her talk in English. With English being the second official language in Tanzania there was no need for a translator. Behind us, whispers could be heard among the little girls. Skylar turned and smiled and the whispers increased until the teacher looked at them and raised her index finger to her lips immediately quieting them. Jane then invited Skylar and me to speak before the class. We introduced ourselves and went on to explain what we were doing with Jane while in Dar. We stressed the importance of caring for their community while still young, and while we believed that it was possible to change some adult's attitudes towards caring for the community, Skylar emphasized that "the habits of children had yet to be fully formed and by reinforcing the importance of respect for one another and their community through education, it will empower *you,* the youth of this and other countries, to successfully carry this message to future generations and potentially heal the world." I will admit this was a pretty heavy message to lay at the feet of these primary school students. Yet despite the gravity in nature of the message, we found ourselves surrounded by eager boys and girls all wanting to know more about Roots and Shoots and their American visitors. One boy told me he wanted very badly to have a pen pal in America, so I offered him my address. His eyes grew wide when I handed the paper to him, and he rushed off to show the others. They gathered around Jeffer, my new pen pal, as he held my address up proudly before them like a trophy, promising the other boys that he would share any letters he received from me.

Skylar, too, found herself surrounded by children. The little girls were in awe of her height. She knelt down to speak with some of the kids while others touched her hair. Skylar waved me over. "This young lady wants to meet you," she said.

"Hello there," I said to the little girl. She just stood smiling, turning away with embarrassment. "Hello," I said again as I reached out for her hand to shake it, "My name is Vince."

"Hello, Vince," she responded. As I stood to walk away, I heard her exclaim to Skylar, "One day I will visit America."

Then a different voice said, "I will never go to America. They call us niggers there and they are mean to black people." His tone told me he really didn't understand what he was saying. As it turned out, he had heard his uncle say this often.

One girl then turned to Skylar, "Is this true?" she asked, clearly hoping that it was not. Skylar looked as if she didn't know how to answer the question. She seemed disgusted by the fact that there was some truth to what the young man had said. She seemed almost ashamed at the answer. Any way she tried to phrase it, the answer still was yes, there were people who considered African-Americans "niggers" and saw them as less human because of their skin color. However, despite this sickening fact, visiting America was a common dream among most of the children we met that day. Though they were aware of the problems of racism that our great nation continued to face, their eyes revealed that America still retained the promise of opportunity and a better life.

I looked around the classroom and saw clusters of children fingering through the pamphlets and discussing what activities they could engage in to help improve their community. Some wanted to do a trash clean-up day for the little creek that ran behind their school. While others said they would collect all the plastic bottles and broken glass and bring it to a local recycling facility. There was even talk of expanding their already existing gardening project and planting more vegetables in order to supply the school cafeteria with vegetables year-round instead of just part of the year. I reflected that of the many papers that both Skylar and I had written as undergrads, it was a simple two page flyer that was proving to have the most impact.

As our time with the students came to an end, we passed out the remaining flyers to students who wanted to give them to their friends. Out of pamphlets and breath, we decided it was time to go. We wished our new friends well and headed back. In the Rover, I felt energized, as if the energy and excitement from those students had rubbed off on me and fed me for the rest of the evening. The next few days were filled with scenes similar to our first one in other primary and secondary schools of Dar as we encouraged kids to join Roots and Shoots and shared our stories of America with a captivated young audience. All too soon, it was time to leave Dar, but the experience of speaking with those children, although brief, would remain with me forever.

PART III

Chapter Eleven

The day greeted me with a smile as I looked out over the balcony and observed the reflection of the sun on the waters of the channel. It was the day we would leave Dar and venture some 600 miles southeast to Kigoma to set up Jane's exhibit. It had taken months of preparation. Jane's team of researchers and volunteers had toiled over numerous details in order to get it just right. Steve brought us to the railroad depot along with a mountain of boxes, protective cardboard tubes, and our suitcases. A railroad attendant quickly rolled his large wooden dolly with hulking metal wheels up to us. Jane and the attendant began to speak in Swahili, and at the conclusion of their brief conversation, he began to quickly load the numerous items onto the dolly. A precarious-looking mound took shape as the attendant desperately attempted to fit everything onto one load. He was keenly aware that this was how he would make the most money, because just as soon as he unloaded our belongings, he could get to another customer and another handsome tip. He was a tiny fellow but possessed the strength of a man four times his size. His ill-fitting trousers bulged at the seams as he squatted to free the dolly from its wooden resting blocks. He proceeded slowly, each step a trembling one as he tried to balance the enormous weight. I walked behind, cheering him in silence as he strained his way the length of ten railcars. We both sighed with relief once the dolly was resting securely again on its wooden blocks, and he began to dismantle the precarious stack, item by item, into the baggage car.

Jane acted like a mother seeing her children off on a distant journey. She was constantly going over what to do if any mishaps occurred, and she kept repeating, "Whatever you do, don't get off the train." She had brought two Scotch bottles that had been emptied of their amber liquid and refilled with water to serve as fragile canteens. "Ration this well, for it is the only water you know is clean while traveling," she warned intently. Thanks to my doctor back home, I was well aware of the various water-borne pathogens that might be lurking. Doctor Armstrong stressed "if you do one thing to keep healthy while traveling, make sure you know the source of your water for it may save your life." Exaggerating or not, I was not about to test his warning, and with Jane's similar words, we both made sure the bottles remained in a cool secure place. She bade us farewell, said, "See you both in Kigoma," and left us standing in the bustling crowd of passengers on the platform. Jane would be journeying by plane and at first I was disappointed the flight was sold out and we could not fly with her. However, the chance to see different parts of East Africa by rail now seemed much more adventurous.

Sky and I ran hand-in-hand as excitement rushed over us like a wave. We searched the dark, slender cars for the number that matched the one on our tickets, and when she spotted it, Skylar proclaimed, "There it is!" as if she were a sailor on watch, calling down at the sight of land. We hurriedly proceeded up the short, steep steps of the railcar. Once inside, we slowed to catch our breath. Sky followed behind me as, still hand-in-hand, we proceeded down the narrow aisle with windows that looked out onto a cluttered platform of people.

When we found our compartment, we swung wide the tiny door and paused to stare at the cramped cabin. To our right was a fairly wide, brown leather bench that traveled the width of the space, roughly two yards. It doubled as a seat during the daylight hours and a bunk at night. Directly above it was a second, foldaway berth that was of comparable length and width to the lower one. There was an efficient set of wooden cabinets covered in a badly chipped white plastic veneer that was built into the wall. Next to it was a sink whose angular base fit snugly into the corner. A chrome fan was bolted above the cabinet and stood motionless as we filed into the restricted space. With both of us standing, nearly all the space was occupied, so I sat down to minimize the claustrophobic feeling building inside me. I sat back into the bottom berth, my weight causing a hissing sound as air seeped from its cushion. The walls were of a light, wood-grained veneer that was cool to the touch as my head rested against it.

Outside, the train's whistle sounded with two bursts; the first one short and the second sustained for several seconds, indicating that we were about to depart. As the conductor eased off the whistle, I was jarred forward and back, causing my head to slam into the wall, and Skylar to fall laughing next to me. "Here we go," I said as the train slowly moved past the platform and out over the span of steel track ahead. The locomotive jerked violently as it desperately tried to remember how to move along the tracks gracefully. The sound of metal striking metal tore at our ears as car couplers banged into one another. Then, as if it had suddenly remembered what to do, the train smoothed out and picked up speed. The harsh sounds were replaced by the cadence of the wheels flowing over the track with a crisp "cha-chink" as they went over the joints in the steel rails.

As we looked out the window of the cabin, the train clanked by villages of concrete and stone blockhouses, some with tin roofs, most with only half of a tin roof and some with no roof at all. Many weeds and other types of random growth sprouted high within the four stone walls of the roofless buildings, which should have been long abandoned but now served as unsafe playgrounds for many of the village's young. I spotted a few children chasing each other through and around the crumbling dwellings. The low-growing vegetation had an appearance similar to the lawn that covered much of the village soil. The only exposed areas of soil I could see were the numerous, neatly cut dirt paths that formed an intricate web of access: house to house, structure to structure, and in and out of the village.

The train's horn sounded and echoed through the landscape as the concrete village slowly shrank into a thick collection of foliage, which seemed reluctant to give up its holding. Now the only things man-made were the seemingly unending string of power poles, which were like toothpicks compared with the massive collection of clumped brush and trees that occupied every inch of the countryside. The whistle blared again. An eerie, lonely echo filled the air and infiltrated the dense growth, causing mass displacement of birds from their perches in towering trees and mountainous brush. These sounds, mixed with the continuous clank of the steel wheels against the track and thick plumes of diesel smoke, created an atmosphere that was new to me and exciting to my senses.

The sun was now hidden behind a few large clouds that filtered its rays and cast them selectively upon nature's mantelpieces. Straining, I stuck my head out the window as far as my neck allowed so as to not miss a single detail of the experience. I noticed the train bending and slithering along the steel rail. At a certain point, we passed through the heart of a mountain that was once whole, but now was divided to allow men to move unfettered across the great distance.

I pondered the great gaps and ravines that once stood as impassable natural barriers, now bridged by steel, wood, and the sweat from a great assembly of workers who had toiled under the merciless conditions of slavery, exposure to the elements, and starvation in order to complete this incredible task many sunrises ago. At its best, the African railroad represented man's victory over nature, the taming of a surly beast, and thus brought about the possibility of covering large distances in times once considered possible only in dreams. It afforded many a man the opportunity to embark upon activities that would reap handsome profits; it also brought family and friends together. At its worst, the African railroad was a permanent reminder of the colonizing Europeans' brutish grasp upon the mighty continent. And like the many slaves they had rounded up, exported, and sold, they had done the same to their land. By bridging and tunneling their way through the rich African earth, the establishment of the railroad meant that no place and no person would be free from the unrelenting grasp of the colonizers.

The train was now traveling at a steady rate, and the passenger cars seemed to sit comfortably upon their wheelbases. I decided to have a look at the other side of the track. Opening my cabin door, I was hit in the face by the smell of human misery. Before me, the entire aisle was packed fore to aft with people with second- and third-class tickets. It was common practice for agents to oversell sitting room aboard the trains, causing passengers to end up packed in the aisles and sometimes the roofs of the train cars.

The crowd of individuals all turned and regarded me with searching eyes, looking me up and down as if trying to locate a piece of clothing, a badge, or something that revealed who I was and what I was doing there. They were mostly men, and most were shirtless. It was only 11:00 a.m. but it was already hot outside, and the clot of bodies confined within the tiny passage produced a heat that was stifling. Those who did keep their shirts on displayed huge sweat stains under their arms, up the middle of their backs, and around their necks. It was a misery solely associated with being poor, since an agent would never dare oversell first-class space on the train. No, this outrageous practice would be tolerated only by those without a means of recourse or refund.

Exiting the cabin, I waded through the passage, tripping over feet and brushing roughly against shoulders until I reached the end of the car. There was an open door, the same door we had used to board the train. The train was now traveling swiftly to Ujiji. The open space beyond the doorway called to me, tempting me to feel the rush by placing my entire body outside a speeding train. Unable to fight the urge, I grasped a railing firmly with my left hand and planted my left foot securely on the coarse metal grating of the stairs, which were situated at the end of each car. I flung myself recklessly into the open air, suspended from certain death only by my grip. Looking down, I watched the earth rush swiftly by my feet as colors blended to form a continuous line. I closed my eyes to experience the sensation of my body fluttering in the swift streams of air shooting past the cars and forcing its way into my lungs.

Suddenly my euphoria was shattered by someone shouting, "Look out!"

I quickly opened my eyes to notice I was inches from a pole of some sort. The start nearly caused me to let go of the railing. Fortunately, my brain responded with an impulse that sent a lightning-fast message to my left arm: *Pull*. The next thing I knew, I was on the floor inside the car and saw the pole whisk by. Breathing heavily, I shook from the adrenaline release. My heart pounded and my ears throbbed from the blood now coursing furiously through my veins, so I could barely hear the laughter. As my breathing slowed, the pounding subsided and I heard clearly chuckling coming from someplace outside. I carefully poked my head out the door again and searched for the source of the laughter. I saw nothing, but heard a voice.

"That was close!" the voice exclaimed, still laughing, and added, "You should have seen your face! Up here," he called to me. There, atop the train's roof, was a man in white clothing sitting with his leg crossed, arms folded across his chest; a large smile revealed crooked front teeth. I thanked him for his warning and told him he had probably saved my life. He introduced himself as Charles and asked me to join him on the roof, pointing to a ladder that ran up the side of each car. I thought about it for a second and declined his offer, saying, "I have had enough excitement for today."

"Oh, come now," he responded. "It is much safer than dangling from the train with your eyes closed. And the view from up here is amazing. You would be surprised at how much more you can see with an extra five feet."

"All right," I said, reaching carefully for the first rung of the ladder and hoisting my body from the safety of the car's floor. Hand over hand, I climbed to the roof. Near the top, the man appeared, leaning over the ladder with an open hand. "Grab on," he instructed as he pulled me up and over onto the dirty black roof. The wind was hot and much stronger up there. Charles sat back down with his legs crossed and arms folded and motioned me over, but I decided to lay face down on the roof for a spell. He didn't mind; he talked anyway. His full, dark lips moved continuously as he explained why he was on the train. Charles was a schoolteacher from Dar. He had taught primary schoolchildren for the past six years and loved it. He had been educated mainly in Tanzania but spent a year abroad at Cambridge University reading English literature. He possessed an amazing arsenal of words, no doubt compliments of Cambridge, and turned out to be an incredibly articulate man. He wore a neatly shorn goatee that accented his shaved head in a way that reminded me of Freud. His wire-rimmed spectacles were angled precariously on his flat nose, and they inched lower with each movement in his face. At times they looked as if they were going to slip off, but he would push them back up. Charles spoke in a manner that one would attribute to a scholar—slowly and methodically. It seemed that each word had value, so he used them sparingly, and he carefully thought through each sentence with amazing clarity and precision. His white clothing flapped in the stream of air as the train clanked over the steel track.

Charles's tone changed when he began to discuss why he was on the train. His wife had recently died of malaria and he was bringing her body to be buried in the village where she had been born. Her family—parents and a younger sister—still lived there and awaited his arrival. He told me he would remain in the village for a few weeks until the burial ritual was complete. I saw an increasing sadness in his eyes, and the continuous talking ceased. The train's air horn blared and filled the vast space around us, which was now mostly dried grass. The mountains had slipped deep into the background, and trees and lush foliage had ceased to exist in this now hostile environment.

I had managed to sit up by this point, and I scooted closer to Charles to offer him support. I placed my hand on his shoulder as his head dipped lower into his chest. He placed his hand atop mine and said, "I had promised you a beautiful view, and all I have shown you is my sadness." He apologized, but I told him not to be ridiculous. I said that if I had lost a wife I truly loved, I would act the same way. His expression suddenly changed once more and I felt his body become tense. He then confided to me that he had not been a good husband and that even though his wife had always expressed her affection for him, he did not return it. He went on to explain how unfairly women were treated throughout Africa. He told me that men could go out and have as many extramarital affairs as they wished, but if a woman behaved in the same manner, the husband could kill her and come away from it with almost no legal or societal repercussions.

Charles related to me that even though he was a respected figure among the schoolchildren and in the community, it had been known and accepted that he was abusive, both physically and mentally, to his wife. He had often felt guilty about his behavior, but he had nowhere to go to express his shame, nor did he have a place to seek help, or so he said. I tried not to show my anger at his admission. I sat quietly listening, and at the conclusion of his confession, he just looked at me, as if awaiting an absolution that I could not give him. We both faced the beautiful display of sky and earth and watched it slip by for nearly an hour.

The sun's light began to wane, telling me I should get back to Skylar. I explained this to Charles and he thanked me for listening. I wished him well. Climbing down, I heard him begin to talk aloud. Thinking he was speaking to me, I climbed back up to take a look. He was now speaking with God. Not wanting to interrupt, I quietly descended the ladder and returned to our cabin. To this day, I hope he finally received the absolution he so desperately sought.

Back in the compartment, Skylar was finishing the final pages of Maya Angelou's book, *I know Why The Caged Bird Sings*. She had read it before, several times in fact, but she claimed to find a new inspirational thought or passage from each reading. Next to her, spread out on the leather berth, was a cloth on which sat two rolls and a cold vegetable samosa, which she had managed to acquire while back at the station, despite our rushing. Sky was always prepared, and this made our adventures more enjoyable. Anything I forgot she brought, and vice versa, although the latter rarely occurred. At the age of twenty, she was already a well-seasoned traveler, having been to most countries in Europe and lived in several Southeast Asian nations as a volunteer with a couple of international aid agencies. Her silky-smooth exterior was deceptive: She could have easily been mistaken for an "indoor girl," but in reality she had spent considerable time in the bush. I had never admired a young woman, let alone loved one. However, I discovered that I was experiencing both these emotions about Skylar.

We sat next to each other and enjoyed our simple meal. Our time in Africa was passing rapidly. Our arrival in Kigoma signified that there were only seven days remaining until we returned to America. In the back of our minds sat the reality that our time together was rapidly passing as well, and still the unresolved future of our relationship remained. Neither of us wanted to summon the topic, so we avoided it quite easily by occupying our conversations with the impending exhibit and our visit to Gombe Stream National Park.

The cabin grew dim as evening descended. I flipped on the cabin's overhead light, only to discover that the buildup of dirt and dust inside the protective cover obscured the bulb's glow. The leather berth cushion hissed as I stepped atop it so I could reach the light. I pushed at the filthy protective cover on the light and carefully removed it, dumping the dust, dirt, and dead bugs out the window. I then rubbed the light's cover with one of my dirty socks and replaced it. The cover didn't smell very good, but it was once again transparent. The bulb now cast its light freely, filling the cabin with its brightness.

Slowly we began preparing for bed. The two of us could barely fit into the same space at the same time, so we took turns. Skylar brushed her teeth at the tiny sink while I got undressed at the other end of the cabin. I pulled off my shirt and draped it neatly over the top of the white-veneered cabinet. I then sat on the berth and pried at my boots. A warm, dank smell arose from my socks, but it was not quite as bad as the smell from the sock I had just used to clean the light, so I judged it had at least one more day of use. I slipped into my cheap plastic sandals and reflected on how essential those ninety-nine-cent sandals had proved to be in combating athlete's foot while on the road.

We switched places. Now I brushed my teeth, using as little of our diminishing water supply as possible, while Skylar changed into a pair of sweats and a T-shirt. We covered the cool leather bench that was to be our bed with a sheet borrowed from Jane's linen cabinet. We pulled the top berth down and threw all our bags on it. Then we both squeezed onto the cozy bottom berth. I could feel the cool leather through the sheet as I scooted to make enough room for Sky. The cool air that blew in from the open window helped to keep the cabin at a perfect temperature, and the melodic clanking over the tracks and the occasional howl of the whistle strangely served as a pacifier for both of us. The coach slightly rocked, and we both drifted into dreams.

Sometime during the night, the train stopped. I was awakened by the cease of pacifying motion, and I lay on my back, staring at the chipped chrome ventilation register on the ceiling while wondering why we weren't moving.

Suddenly I heard a furious pounding on our cabin door. I shot up quickly and my head crashed into the top berth. I stumbled to my feet, rubbing my forehead in pain, and threw on the light. The pounding continued and the door creaked, weakening under the blows. Opening the door, I found a man who resembled a rabid dog. His lips curled and writhed around his gums, exposing his jagged teeth. His mouth moved in a barking manner. I was still half-asleep and half-dazed from knocking my head, so everything appeared to happen in slow motion. He was shouting in Swahili, which added to the already surreal scene. He realized I was out of it, so he pushed his way past me. I could see that he was bristling with anger at me. "But why?" I asked myself. He was ugly and had a ferocious temperament that matched his ugliness on all counts. I wondered what type of woman could give birth to such a vile human being, and I knew that even under the best of circumstances, I would still dislike this man.

The beast went straight to our open window. He turned, showed his teeth, and shouted in English, "Don't open dis window!" I didn't answer; I just looked deep into his eyes as my anger built. He sensed his intimidation card was played out. He quickly followed up his sentence, explaining that bandits moved about on the roofs of the train cars, sneaking into the open windows of unsuspecting passengers to rob and kill them. He moved his huge pointer finger across his thick neck in a slicing motion. He turned back to the window, slammed it closed, and secured it by wedging a piece of wood under it. Then he pushed past me again and slammed our door. I locked it.

Skylar laughed nervously as I sat next to her on the berth. That asshole may have saved our lives, but I resented his lack of civility and level of attempted intimidation. Suddenly, the train jerked several times and began to lurch forward. We were relieved to be moving again and laid back into the security and comfort of our berth.

The morning brought a welcome brightness along with pleasant aromas of food cooking. The train stopped again, but this time it was a scheduled stop for food. As for last night's mysterious stop, it turned out to be for repairs on the diesel engine.

I was still a bit shaken from the previous evening's encounter with the conductor, and Skylar suggested that a nice breakfast would put me at ease. We opened the cabin door to find the aisle empty of its human cargo. The standing passengers, like us, had decided to disembark the train to take a stroll on solid ground and enjoy some hot food. When I stepped from the train onto the pea-size gravel, it shifted under my weight, almost causing me to fall. I regained my balance but felt stiff and sluggish, as if blood weren't circulating properly through my body. I stretched upwards into the sky with both arms, reaching as far as my bone and tissue allowed. As I released the stretch, the tension and stiffness began to leave my body. I repeated this several times. Skylar stretched as well, concentrating on her legs because the cramped quarters and lack of movement had made her knees hurt.

By now the pleasant aromas of grilling meat and seasoned rice had become so intense that we could not think of any other activity but eating. Small children carried wooden skewers with pieces of chicken, beef, or a combination of both. These succulent meats filled every inch of the spearlike lengths of wood. I purchased two for about thirty cents. Warm juices dripped off the meat onto my hand. They smelled wonderful, thrusting my salivary glands into overdrive, forcing me to take a bite. The chicken was tender, and each chew released an unfamiliar, sweet, smoky flavor. It was delicious. I tried the beef too, which was also tender, but had a zestier, almost sour taste. It was also delicious. From the corner of my eye, I spotted a pair of eyes locked on my food. I walked over and gave the beef skewer to an old man sitting in one of the abandoned boxcars located on a set of tracks that detoured from the main line. "*Asante,*" he said, smiling and bowing his hairless head repeatedly in gratitude.

In between the abandoned boxcars and the train was a strip of open space, and this was where the grills stood. There were several of them. Each was supported by thin, metal legs, which raised it approximately four feet above ground level. The grills were mainly constructed of scrap metal from the abandoned boxcars punctuated by numerous holes to let the heat and smoke rise through them. They were kept clean with large wire brushes that hung from the side. Behind each grill stood a man or woman cooking. White smoke rose from the smoldering wood and enveloped the cooking meats, while a layer of grease from prior use slowly melted from the intense heat and dripped occasionally into the grill, sizzling and encouraging a flame to jump, which added to the already delightful aroma. Next to the searing meats were large pots of freshly boiled rice, resting on an area of the grill that kept it warm enough to eat but didn't allow it to burn. A crusty, black residue stuck to the outside of these pots from where the flames had licked at them. Steam seeped from tiny openings in the lids of the pots, allowing the starchy smell from the rice to join in the chorus of wonderful smells.

I walked up to a man behind one of the grills. He wore a dark pair of trousers and a yellow collared shirt, clothing that would look more appropriate behind a desk than at a barbecue grill. He stood with a smile and his hands worked magically as he turned, basted, and moved the meats regularly about the grill. "Two bowls of rice, please," I asked. He continued to smile as he quickly scooped steaming rice, flavored with chicken and beef drippings, into two Styrofoam bowls. The combined heat from the grill and the sun caused sweat to bead and roll frequently from his forehead onto his nose and cheeks. And his eyes watered from the continuous exposure to the thick, white smoke. Despite this discomfort, he kept a smile on his face. I watched all of this while devouring my skewer of chicken, and I ordered two more skewers.

Not all of the outdoor grills were for cooking food, however. About 10 yards away, Skylar stood in front of dozens of dented, aluminum kettles atop these grills as the aroma of steeping tea mixed with the others. I walked over to observe the operation and then a woman touched my arm to stop me. She added a spoonful of dark honey to the tea she had poured into a bottle, screwed on the top, turned to me, and raised the bottle with two hands. I just held up the skewers of chicken and bowls of rice letting her know my hands were full and I could not accept it. Plus I had no idea where that water came from. She nodded with understanding, and we returned to the cabin. We sat in our room and enjoyed our meal as the morning sun filled the tiny space with cheerful light. I placed handful after handful of rice into my mouth as the moist grains, saturated with drippings, satiated my hunger.

Outside, passengers were everywhere, talking, stretching, buying, napping in the sun, or laughing. The train journey was two-thirds complete, and by three that afternoon we would be in Kigoma. The excitement of arriving and disembarking the train naturally preoccupied everyone's thoughts. Traveling is always difficult, but in a developing country it can be a nightmare. It didn't bother me so much, but it must have been a real hardship on the mothers with small children. I watched one mother trying to comfort her two bawling children just outside my cabin window. Both appeared to have weeping rashes on their bare bottoms. She sought some privacy by the abandoned boxcars and rubbed a soothing salve onto each rash. Suddenly the train's whistle sounded, one short blast followed by a long one, signifying the engineer's readiness to depart. The mother dressed her children and quickly walked with them, hand in hand, to their car. I followed them with my eyes until they disappeared into a third-class coach. Seconds later, the train jerked forward. Metal-on-metal squeaks sounded down the line of cars as we continued rolling toward our destination.

It was now close to noon. The mercury had climbed to dizzying heights as the sun beat down on the dirty, black roofs of the railcars. Inside we sweltered like never before. Skylar and I took turns sticking our heads out the window, but even this provided little respite from the heat. The streams of air were hot and humid and almost choked us. I had removed my shirt some fifty miles back. Skylar had only a bra and panties on. She was very sensitive to extreme heat. She soaked a bandanna and placed it over her head, letting the excess water drip onto her shoulders and down her back and chest. The environment outside was arid and grew less hospitable to life with every passing minute. The lush greens had faded to mostly brown and beige vegetation. Nothing stirred outside in the hostile climate, and nothing stirred inside the train. Many conserved energy by remaining still, hoping for a quick arrival into Kigoma and the cooler temperatures that evening would bring. By three, our anticipated arrival time, we were still nearly two hours from Kigoma.

The train had now slowed to a crawl. I grew frustrated, and along with this feeling sprang anger. Skylar had managed to take a nap while I sat near the window cursing everyone from the engineer right down to the aging diesel equipment. I quickly left the cabin, seeking solace in visiting my friend, Charles, on the roof. I climbed the ladder only to find he was no longer on this roof, nor on the roofs of the cars immediately connected. Disappointed, I returned to my cabin. However, on my way back, I noticed the calm manner of the people in the aisle of the train car. Surely they, too, were upset with the delay in arrival. They had had no seat, no privacy, and no bed to lie on for more than twenty-four hours. Yet they remained calm and displayed the discipline of well-trained soldiers. I, on the other hand, acted like an impatient child. Ashamed, I felt my anger, frustration, and impatience leave me as abruptly as if the wind had been socked out of me.

With an enlightened attitude, I returned to the cabin. Sitting atop the small sink, I rested my arms on the open window frame and watched the scene change as we rumbled slowly along the tracks. Suddenly I spotted a young man reaching his long, slender arms up to each window of the car as it passed by his position on the ground. In each hand he held a carved wooden plane. Obviously he was selling them, and if the person inside the car was interested, he or she would call to the young man and he would jog alongside the crawling train until a deal was made. I leaned against the window and watched him work his way toward me. Then I noticed other vendors as well, and I wondered how they all knew we would be traveling at this slow speed at this particular spot. I then wondered if this was a planned agreement between the engineer and the vendors, because there were too many of them for this to be a coincidence.

There were scores of vendors selling all sorts of carved wooden objects, from airplanes to three-legged stools. It must have been lucrative because I saw many a vendor's hands exchanging merchandise for passengers' money. Curious to see their work, I whistled to the young boy with the airplanes. He came running over, along with another kid who also carried planes. There was a brief spat between them, then the second boy turned and walked away. I asked to see one of the planes, and the vendor handed it to me. I knew I had just bought that plane whether I wanted it or not. Luckily it was a nice piece of work; it had tiny carved windows and tiny wooden wheels for the landing gear, and intricate patterns and shapes had been branded into the wings and body. The boy blew on the propellers of the plane he was holding and they spun with ease on tiny wing mounts. Laughing, I asked, "How much?" I was pretty sure he spoke English, but he chose to use his fingers to indicate a price. He raised five fingers and made two zeros with the other hand. "Five hundred!" I exclaimed.

"That's too much," Skylar spoke up from behind.

"Four hundred," I offered. He shook his head in refusal as he slowly jogged alongside the moving train. He then motioned me to look at the detail and craftsmanship of the plane in my hand again. I broke down and went with the five hundred shillings, which came out to roughly a dollar and a half. I reached in my wallet and found only three hundred shillings. I then looked into my knapsack for a couple of dollars. All I had were twenties. I didn't have the heart to tell him I didn't have the right bills. After all the running he had done to keep pace with the train, I felt he had earned the sale. I grabbed a twenty and handed it to him through the window. His eyes grew as big as a tennis balls and he offered me the other plane. Politely, I declined. Then he ran over to a boy selling three-legged stools, grabbed one, caught up to my window and held it up to me with two hands. "Please," he said, "take this." I hesitated, then smiled and reached down to grab my new stool. "*Asante*, thank you," he shouted as he finally stopped running with the train. Exchanged on the black market, that U.S. twenty would fetch him nearly ten times the price he had asked for his plane. He continued to wave as I watched a few of his friends gather around him to share in his good fortune. I waved as he got smaller and smaller, then disappeared.

Chapter Twelve

The first thing I did upon arriving at the Kigoma station was to slip into a bar located right up the street. Sitting under an arbor of freshly cut mango leaves, sipping from a cold bottle of lager, I watched the hordes of passengers disembark the overcrowded train. Jane was there to meet us at the station. She had flown, and now I knew why. Skylar remained with Jane while I snuck away for a drink and some relief from the crowds. The scene upon arrival was similar to departure—noisy and crowded. Some people wandered around, confused, trying to figure out where to go next, while others were embraced in the arms of waiting wives, husbands, sons, and daughters. From my chair on the bar's patio, I searched for my new friend, Charles, but I did not see him. I started to think he had gotten off at one of the stops we'd made during the night because Kigoma was the last stop on the rail line from Dar. I never saw him again after our short time on the roof together.

Kigoma had a wide dirt road running through the center of town. On either side were huge, shady mango trees that were reminiscent of the elms and maples lining the streets of America during the 1950s. For being the most important port of Lake Tanganyika, it was very slow-paced and exactly the type of atmosphere I was craving after the draining twenty-seven-hour train journey. I watched an occasional truck roll by with a United Nations insignia stenciled on the doors. Among other things, Kigoma housed a thriving community of aid agencies from all over the world and had numerous programs targeted at development. "They are everywhere," spouted a raspy voice from the corner of the patio. I turned to my left to see a thin white man in jeans and a white T-shirt that read CARE in blue letters.

"What's that?" I asked.

"U.N. trucks," he said, pointing to the street as another one rolled by. "They're everywhere."

I told him he must have read my mind because that was exactly what I was thinking. He explained that was the second thing he had noticed upon arriving in Kigoma some five years ago. The first thing he had noticed, of course, were the beautiful, shady mango trees. He introduced himself as Boo and told me he had left his job as a freelance writer in New York to, in his words, "get away from it all." He arrived in Nairobi and took a journey similar to ours, from Nairobi to the Serengeti, then to Dar, and finally Kigoma. For money, he did contract jobs for different agencies. Because of his familiarity with the area and his proficiency in local languages, he was sought after and was rarely without a job or money. Boo told me he gave away half of his salary to various people he knew, and the other half he spent on lager and black market whiskey. He drank the remaining part of his lager and let out a sound of satisfaction. "Want another one?" he asked, pointing to my empty bottle. I accepted his offer, and we ended up having another, as well as four more after that. "To development!" he declared in his raspy voice. I laughed and took a refreshing swallow of my brew.

Boo had a love-hate relationship with the aid agencies and commonly referred to them as "necessary evils in a world of evil." He worked for them year after year, but he felt all his work was in vain. He felt the place was still the same as it had been five years earlier. "Hell, if you ask some of the other aid cronies, they'll give some song and dance and whip out charts that monitor improvement and all that bullshit." He chuckled deeply and began to cough, then spit onto the patio floor. "I tell ya, I determine improvement by what I see, and I still see the same one-road town." Boo then broke into a coughing fit. He covered his mouth tightly, and his pale face turned scarlet from the force of his coughs. He began sweating, though there was no real heat to speak of. The shady trees kept everything comfortable. I went and asked the barkeep for a bottle of water and brought it to him. He thanked me and drank it down. He wiped the hand covering his mouth across his faded jeans, and I noticed small traces of blood. I knew Boo was ill, but I did not quiz him about it. No, he was enjoying his time and continued to speak.

With no wife or children, Boo was free to roam as he pleased and often took months out of the year to trek about the continent. In fact, he had been back only two days from Nigeria when I met him. I was interested in the specifics of his various contract jobs and asked what types of programs he had worked on.

"Off the top of my head," he said, "there was the lend/lease program for the fishermen of Lake Tanganyika." He explained this was a program in which fishing nets and outboard motors were lent to the fishermen with the notion that once they had made enough money, they would pay back the costs of the equipment. However, this program was proving to be a failure on two key points—repayment and "collateral damage," as he put it. First, the fishermen rarely, if ever, paid back the cost of the nets and motors. The most they ever did was return broken motors and nets full of holes. Second, a new engine and net would be provided to whoever showed up with a boat, usually a handmade canoe, increasing the amount of fishermen on the lake by nearly one hundred percent in one year. The overfishing of Africa's largest freshwater lake had now become a problem. And when the fishing stock in deeper waters was depleted, the fishermen came in closer to the shore and netted the smaller fish, which disturbed the nurseries.

"If these questionable methods persist," he said, "the fish population will drop to dangerously low levels, affecting not only the survival of man but also the survival of other creatures in the immediate ecosystem." According to Boo, the U.N. had planned a vigorous campaign to raise the population of fish. They discussed imposing a six-month moratorium on fishing the lake, and then once the lake was repopulated, they would impose yearly poundage limits, confident this would keep the number of fish in the lake at sustainable levels.

The reason for lending the nets and outboard motors was to increase productivity among fishermen so two pressing issues could be addressed: first, feeding the residents in the immediate area, and second, providing the fishermen with a steady source of income. This, of course, was part of an overall plan to further develop and stabilize an economic base for the community, helping it to become and remain self-sufficient.

Another program was the development of small economic enterprises by offering loans to women for the purpose of starting their own businesses. This, too, aimed at assisting individuals to generate personal income and strengthen the local economic base. They started businesses that related to the local fishing economy, becoming purveyors of fish oils for cooking as well as other products. "Most of the women did well in business for themselves, and what made this program a total success was the payback rate of these loans. Of all the loans made to women, nearly ninety-three percent of them were paid back within two years," Boo stated, appearing excited about his recollection. And for a moment, the sarcasm and bitterness left his voice as his idealist roots, which had dried up so many years back, suddenly came to life again. "Compare this with the men's average I mentioned, and one quickly deduces who is the more honest of the two species," Boo stated as the hoarseness of his voice increased, and he poured the last sip of his lager down to moisten his dry throat.

"So, what's your story?" he asked, clearing his throat. "What brings you to Kigoma?" I told him about Jane and the exhibit we would be doing. I even invited him to it. He was speechless for a moment, then smiled like a little kid being asked to come and play. "I'd like that," he replied coolly. We shook good-bye.

I walked to the exhibition site, praying that Jane and Skylar hadn't left yet. Picking up my pace, I could hear Boo coughing the hardest yet. I turned around to help him. However, the barkeep had already come to his aid. By the looks of the situation, the barkeep had helped him before. Since Boo had lived in Kigoma for five years, I figured the barkeep was probably a friend of his. He knelt next to Boo and patted him on the shoulder softly, saying, "Easy, man," over and over. He then gave Boo a damp cloth to wipe the blood from his hands. Boo thanked him by name, confirming my notion that they were friends. He ordered another lager and started over again. I think he hoped the booze would kill him before the illness did.

Continuing toward the exhibit site, I heard "Vince" to my distant left. It was Skylar; she and Dr. Jane, who arrived to greet us, were standing by the open door of our train's baggage coach. A conductor appeared from the open door and spoke to Dr. Jane. I couldn't make out what he said, but Jane's reply was "Oh, dear."

As I got closer, Skylar asked, "Where have you been?" in a concerned manner.

"I'm sorry," I immediately replied. "Hello Jane, I hope you had a nice flight over." I said as I gave her a welcoming hug. I then turned back to Skylar, "I thought you heard me when I told you I was going over to that café for a drink," I explained, though I was not really sure if I did, indeed, tell her where I was going. She didn't press the matter any further. Instead, she explained that a few of our boxes were missing. They had been moved in order to make room for the other passengers' luggage, and now nobody knew where they were. "It gets worse," she added. "The boxes contained the pamphlets and the replicas of the chimpanzee tools we spent so many hours making."

"You're kidding me!" I replied, shocked. "All that work everyone did for this exhibition, for nothing!" I exclaimed in frustration.

Jane quickly responded to my frustration. "Don't worry Vince, they will turn up, I'm just not sure when", she said with a slight giggle. "What do we do about the exhibit?" I asked rubbing the back of my head. "The children who are expecting us, oh I hate to let them down." Skylar added. But the reality was that without the material we had no exhibit. And Jane confirmed this but also added that more than likely the material would turn up in the next couple of weeks and that the exhibit could be carried out at that time. Jane admitted the students at the school that was hosting the exhibit would be disappointed but the knowledge that it would be carried out at a later date would help to ease their disappointment.

At that point we made our way to the exhibit site. It was a long barn-type structure made from concrete with rows of large windows on both sides. The structure was not part of the school but because of its close proximity to the school, it was used as an assembly area for plays, and musical performances performed by the students. I peeked through an open iron door. A row of chairs stacked five high was neatly against the back wall in anticipation of our exhibit, and the display tables that should have been set up had the material arrived with us.

Jane, was across the way from us about a hundred yards and meeting with the headmaster under a large shade tree just outside his office. By his expressions he was not upset that the exhibit would have to be delayed, in fact he was smiling and had his hand on Jane's right shoulder seeming to assure her that everything would work out. And with that, Dr. Jane shook his hand and walked over to where we were standing. "Such a nice fellow," she stated. "He completely understood our situation and that it was not our fault. Coincidently," she added, "a few weeks back he had expected some test booklets to arrive via train that didn't. However two days later the books came. He was very reassuring and told me that when the material arrives we can plan the exhibit then. Such a nice fellow!" she said again.

The three of us left the school and made our way back toward the train station, or at least I thought we were heading toward the train station and would return to Dar. However, Jane had something else in mind. "I know you two are disappointed that you put in all that work for an exhibition you will not be able to see since you are leaving in a couple of days, so how about rather than returning to Dar we go visit Chimpanzees?" She questioned with a smile. Skylar and I immediately brightened up like shooting stars and answered simultaneously, "Absolutely!" See, we had not expected to visit the Chimpanzees with Jane because we were all so busy getting the roots and shoots material ready for school visits and the exhibit in Kigoma. As fate would have it, the display material not arriving proved to be a good thing because we would now have extra time to go and see where Dr. Jane's lifelong research was launched! We were giddy with excitement and questions for Jane as we caught a taxi to a boat launch to begin the last and most unexpected leg of our journey.

Chapter Thirteen

Making our way to the boat launch, an occasional structure could be seen peeking out from the thick green
foliage on both sides of the road. Soon the uneven-
ness of the foliage began to smooth out like a blanket of green
and brown. The blanket covered the entire landscape as it began
to gradually ramp upwards until it stopped at dramatic cliffs.
These steep walls of earth went straight down to the water in
some areas, while in others the walls rolled gently downward
until they reached the lapping waves of the lake. Resting neatly
atop the cliff was a community of houses. They were pushed
well back from the edge and formed a neat row that tipped
slightly upward, accenting the top of the cliff. They were sturdy
houses built of all interlocking concrete blocks painted white
with bright red-tiled roofs and peaceful unobstructed views of
the lake. It was a wonderful departing picture as the boat left.

Gombe Stream National Park lay roughly twelve miles to the
north of Kigoma. The tiny boat powered its way through the
choppy waters of Lake Tanganyika with ease. The droning of
the outboard motor filled my ears as we traveled along the shore
of the lake to Gombe. The bow, lifted by a wave, came up out of
the water and then dropped back down through the empty
space left by the passing wave until it slammed onto the water's
surface. In order to smooth the ride out a bit, our guide, Jumanne
Kikwale, maneuvered closer to the shore, but this did little to
decrease the tossing motion of the restless waters.

To the right now ran a narrow, sandy shore with a row of

trees that grew roughly twenty-five yards back from the water's edge. The row of trees formed a dense but narrow green wall that ran parallel to us for some distance. Behind the cluster of trees lay dozens of hills. These huge, rolling mounds of earth filled the background of Lake Tanganyika's shore. Staring in awe at the magnificent collection of hills, it struck me that they looked out of place, for rather than being green with growth, they were almost entirely devoid of it. It was a scene from the desert, not the basin of a freshwater lake.

I asked Jummane Kikwale, a longtime worker at Gombe, "What happened to the trees?" He informed me that some had been cut down to use as fuel or as lumber for building houses, but the majority of the trees were cut down to make way for the planting of crops.

"See those trees over there?" he asked, pointing to a section of hills in the Gombe reserve that was thick with lush, green foliage. "That is what all these hills should look like!" He went on to reinforce his previous statement and said, "The deforestation was primarily a by-product of the local farmers' planting crops and using an ancient method called *terrace farming* used in many parts of the world. They used this method to compensate for the lack of level ground in the surrounding areas thinking it would provide and answer for the growing need for food production. Farmers cut down all the trees and cleared all the brush, leaving the hillside bare. They then plowed the soil and planted their crops. When done correctly it works beautifully and crops flourish but unfortunately the drainage was not done correctly here. I think it was just too steep. When the rainy season came, the intense rainfall washed all the loosened topsoil and crops right into the lake." Jummane continued to explain, "In addition to causing large amounts of erosion, it proved to have minimal benefits for local food production and in fact produced less at times due to the erosion. The have finally stopped this practice in this area, but as you can see the damage is done, and it will take years to repair, if ever there is money to be spent on such a thing," Jummane concluded in a discouraged manner.

Next to Jummane, near the middle of the boat, sat Jane. Her eyes were closed and her body moved up and down. She was one with the rocking craft. With her head tilted back, she exposed her relaxed face to the soft light from the late-afternoon sun. The lapels of her white-collared shirt fluttered slightly in the breeze. Behind her sat a barefoot young man in his late teens. He had taken over for Jummane. He sat with one hand on the tiller while the other tightly grasped the side of the boat. He squinted alertly forward, making sure we were on course. Jummane watched the youth intently, making sure that he was attentive, and he was doing fine.

The lake's water was a rich hue of blue, and it thudded as it hit the stern of the wooden boat. The rocking continued, but luckily I wasn't feeling any motion sickness. Skylar, on the other hand, was sick. By now the olive tone of her skin had turned green. I asked if she was alright, and she replied by asking me to grab hold of her wrist and keep a constant pressure in the place where one usually checks for a pulse. She had read in some medical journal that this eases even the most severe bouts of motion sicknesses. I held her wrist and applied pressure with my thumb. She swayed with the movement of the boat, her eyes tightly closed as if trying desperately to concentrate on something other than the bouncing boat. The boat's motor had a steady drone that was occasionally broken when going over a large wave. The drone became a high-pitched whine that caused me to grit my teeth. It was an unsettling noise similar to that of someone raking fingernails down a chalkboard.

After ten minutes of steady pressure, the edges of Skylar's mouth on her once expressionless face began to curve upwards. She opened her eyes and declared softly, "It's working." I continued with the pressure and began to smile. Things were good as we made our way along the shore of Lake Tanganyika.

Suddenly the hills stretching along the shoreline were once again covered in a lush green tangle of trees and brush. This was where the fifty-two kilometers of Gombe Stream National Park began and the ugliness of deforestation ended. As we grew closer to shore, the tangle of foliage came to life with the exotic sounds of wildlife that lay hidden in the growth. The barefoot young man quickly made his way to the stern of the vessel, climbing over Skylar and me, and dropped anchor. The *kerplunk* of the metal anchor was followed by a short length of chain clanking over the side of the boat until it hit bottom and fell silent.

There on the shores of Gombe two of Jane's research assistants, Bill and Charlotte, greeted us. "Welcome back," they said to Jane, smiling and receiving her as if their matriarch had returned. They welcomed Skylar and me with handshakes, then handed each of us a small glass with about an inch of single-malt. We graciously accepted their offer. Then all of us, with a glass in hand, sat down for a while to talk as we anticipated the setting sun.

The beach on this particular section of shore was not sand, but was composed of tiny stones, not big enough to actually hurt one's bare feet, but not small enough to be totally comfortable. I achieved some measure of comfort by scooting the small stones around a bit with my bottom and then sitting in the recess I had created. The lake's water now appeared white as the sun's light reflected off the surface. In the distance, a slight haze made it appear as if the lake went on for many miles, then just disappeared into the abyss. I had never seen a lake so big that it actually reminded me of an ocean. Skylar and I now sat as close together as we possibly could. With her arms clasped tightly around my shoulders, we engaged in conversation with the others.

The sun began to make its final descent behind the earth. The huge glowing ball contained a mixture of white and orange bursts of color and dipped lower with each passing second.

Lower and lower it went as sections vanished until it was gone and only its powerful afterglow remained. Bill, who noticed that Skylar and I were locked in a tight embrace, held up his glass and toasted us for watching a Gombe sunset the way it should be watched—with someone you love. "Welcome to Gombe," he added, and the last of the single-malt disappeared into his mouth. We all drained our glasses, then retreated into the house to begin preparing the evening's dinner.

Behind us, about twenty-five yards from the lake and up a slight rise, sat the concrete-block house that we would call home for the next three days. As we approached it, a set of steps brought us onto the front porch. It had a concrete floor protected by a pitched tin overhang that was supported by a mishmash of sturdy wooden beams. The perimeter of the porch was wrapped in a low cement wall that had rectangular holes spaced evenly along the bottom, to allow water to escape, I assumed. I looked up at the tin overhang to see if there were any holes in it. There were no holes, just tiny rust spots that dotted its underside. In the wall that separated the house from the porch, there were two large, square holes on either side of the doorway. Each square was framed by wood and had a wooden divider that ran through the center of the opening, giving it a window-like appearance. Instead of glass, the opening held sturdy wire mesh. This helped to keep the larger critters out, I'd find out later, but was ineffective for mosquitoes.

Inside the wooden doorway, the space opened up into a large living area. At one end of the room, under a window opening, sat a couch with a round table in front of it. Directly to my left was a beat-up file cabinet that appeared to have been made by someone who had no woodworking skills whatsoever, which made the wide wooden chair next to it appear to be a finely crafted piece of furniture. A small bookcase with three or so shelves rested against the back wall of the house and was stuffed beyond capacity with books of all sizes. The stucco walls had been covered with a yellowing whitewash that had brown traces or stains wherever the wood met concrete. The concrete floor was clean and smooth and had a grayish-white tint.

On the other end of the room was the cooking area, complete with a set of burners that ran on kerosene and an indoor fire pit that vented out of one of the two front window openings. Wooden countertops conveniently surrounded the cooking area. Of course, there was no need for a sink for washing up. When finished with a meal, one could simply rinse the dishes clean with the fresh lake water. On the shelves sat a sparse assortment of nonperishables: peanut butter, *Vegemite*, *McCann's* oatmeal, UHT milk, tea, sugar, and so on. In fact, one of the first things Skylar and I did was to unpack the groceries that Jane had purchased in Kigoma. We restocked the shelves and refrigerator with pasta, rice, fresh bread, vegetables, fruits, a few bars of chocolate and a nice hunk of cheese at which Bill almost wept when Jane showed it to him. He thanked her with a quick peck on the cheek, went over to the counter, pulled out a large knife, and proceeded to cut himself a piece. "Mmm," Bill sighed with delight.

Jane showed us to our room. We walked through a doorway from the cooking area into a first bedroom, then went on through another doorway into our bedroom. It was a spacious room with a desk tucked neatly in the corner by a window opening that looked out onto the lake. The bed, which rested against the long wall that divided the first bedroom from ours, consisted of two pieces of foam, each the size of a single mattress, placed next to each other and covered by a large sheet. This makeshift mattress rested upon a sheet of plywood that was raised about two feet from the ground by concrete blocks. I placed my suitcase and backpack on the floor, then lay diagonally across the bed to test its comfort. The bed, like the house, proved to be quite deceptive. The cinder-block house looked small from the outside, but inside it proved to be quite spacious. And although the bed looked as if it would be uncomfortable, once I laid across it, it proved to be fine. Above the bed hung a mosquito net that was suspended precariously by two thin pieces of rope that hung from one wall to the other. It wasn't the Hilton, but it was no less comfortable.

Chapter Fourteen

The penetrating sound of an electronic buzzer was my first registered sound of the day. It was morning, but the sun was not yet up. I rolled over and shook Skylar, whose sleep had not been broken by the buzzer. Reaching out to the blackened lantern next to the bed, I used my fingers to twist a thin metal knob that slowly raised the kerosene-soaked wick. With a strike of a match, the lantern was now glowing, and it chased the darkness from our room. I rose and slipped into a pair of warm wool socks. My olive khakis were next. Bare-chested, I grabbed a towel I had draped over the chair in the corner and put on my cheap plastic sandals. I lit a second lantern and took this one with me as I stumbled toward the front door. The air outside was a few degrees warmer, but still crisp. As I made my way to the lake, the tiny stones made a crunching sound with each step. There, at the water's edge, the stones were reduced to not-quite-fine granules of sand, but it was sand nonetheless. Small, gentle waves made a distinct lapping sound. The sky was dark, but with the light around the edges, one knew it was only a matter of minutes before the darkness would give way to day.

I set the towel down and sat on it, removed my sandals, and rolled up my khakis. Stepping into the cold water sent a shock through my body, helping to eliminate any remaining grogginess. I splashed the water onto my face and hair. Knowing that soap would be harmful to marine life, I picked up a handful of the granules from the shore and slowly began to cleanse my face with them. The combination of the fresh lake water and the sand scrub left me feeling energized and ready to search for chimps. Walking back to the house, I could see several kerosene lamps burning in different parts of the house, and through the windows saw that Bill and Skylar were now up.

As I entered the house, I found Bill sitting in the wide chair by the door. Leaning forward to tie his shoes, he told me he had boiled some water Sky and I could use to make tea or oatmeal. Skylar now entered the room. "Good morning," she said to Bill and me, just above a whisper, careful not to wake the others. I suddenly realized that for the first time since arriving in Tanzania, I was up before Jane. Skylar and I quickly poured and finished a cup of tea and sliced ourselves some bread. Bill, already outside, stood on the shore of the lake and stared out over the water. We walked up quietly behind him.

"Beautiful, isn't it?" he said.

"Sure is," Skylar responded.

"Oh, yeah," I agreed.

"Are you ready to get started?" Bill asked. We once more answered in the affirmative. "Let's go un-nest some chimpanzees!" he declared in a tone so full of enthusiasm one would have thought this was his first time at Gombe.

Not ten minutes passed before we were in the thick of the foliage of Gombe. Bill forged roughly twenty yards ahead. Effortlessly he powered up the narrow dirt path, which lay completely covered with brown leaves. The constant forty-five degree climb hammered away at Skylar and me until we were gasping for breath. When the distance between us and Bill grew too great, he would stop just long enough to hear our noisy footsteps or our labored breathing before moving on again. The brush became so dense in some areas that the sun's early light was almost blocked out. These were the scariest parts of the trek, as far as I was concerned, because it was hard to see what you were stepping onto or what you were touching for support. Bill rarely spoke while on the hike, and if he did, it was usually a warning. For instance, in one steep section of the climb that was thick with brush, he instructed, "Watch closely what you grab onto overhead when pulling yourself up, because snakes can hang out in vegitation and if you grab a snake instead of a branch, it could be deadly."

Bill, undaunted by these dangers, continued to drive steadily through the thick underbrush. His olive-drab trousers and matching vest caused him at times to blend into the surrounding snarl of growth. His black turf shoes gave him just enough traction to quickly conquer steep passages, while Skylar and I slipped continuously on the moist, slippery earth. Bill would stop and turn, looking at us with a smile on his face, often asking if we were okay—his boldness hadn't yet callused the gentle side of his personality.

In certain areas, he would stop suddenly and raise his right hand to halt Skylar and me dead in our tracks. He listened intently to any movement or sound that might give away where the chimps were. The morning light grew brighter with every passing minute until the early-morning light had become full-blown daylight. This did not bode well for us in our attempt to find nesting chimpanzees. Bill informed us that our chances of finding sleeping chimps were fleeting, and that more than likely they were already awake and on the move, looking for food and a new place to nest for the coming night.

Skylar and I were not disappointed, though, and we conveyed to Bill that just being in Gombe and attempting to un-nest the chimps was exciting; whether or not we actually succeeded was not a concern. Bill seemed impressed by our genuine but undemanding excitement. He knew our spirits could not be dampened because being in Gombe was reward enough.

The earth was cold and damp, and there were many sections of the trail where we were on our hands and knees in order to follow the same path that the chimps would use. The knees of my khakis were soiled through, and a deep brown color now replaced the drab olive. I could feel the penetrating coldness on the flesh of my knees. My hands grew numb from constant contact with the damp earth. Crawling on my hands and knees, I would regularly have to pause and scrape a layer of mud from my palms.

I sensed Bill was growing frustrated that we hadn't sighted any chimps yet. We repeatedly seemed to arrive in an area that the chimps had just left. Trampled leaves, broken branches, and half-nibbled goodies were all we saw.

We continued to comb the brush-laden inclines, following the lead of a determined Gombe veteran. Only two hours had passed since we had set out on this adventure, and already the muscles in my legs were screaming in pain. The rest of my body too rebelled against this laborious hike by sending shooting pains through my back, neck, and ankles. I guess my body was trying to tell me to stop. But I couldn't; I had to keep up. I didn't want to disappoint Bill, nor did Skylar. I could tell by her stride that her running injuries were hounding her like an overbearing mother; however, she wasn't about to stop either. In fact, when I asked if she was tired, she firmly stated "No" and added something feisty about how this reminded her of a good cross-country course back home.

We now surfaced from the thick underbrush and treaded upon a wider path that opened up to a brilliant, blue sky. By now the sun's rays had warmed the surrounding air to a comfortable temperature.

We had climbed our way out of the cellar, so to speak, and now, rather than looking up at everything, we were looking over everything. Hills surrounded us and were thick with tree cover that seemed to be endless, at least as far as I could see. The muscles in my legs swelled with blood that furiously transported oxygen to them. My steps were now reduced to a gait that was barely above dragging. I prayed for a second wind, and when that didn't come, a miracle. I prayed for anything that would cause us to cease our ascent.

Suddenly Bill stopped. I thought this unusual because neither of us had fallen, nor had we drifted out of earshot. As Skylar and I drew closer, he told us we would rest here briefly. My prayer had been answered as I sat on the fallen leaves and stretched my sore legs out before me. Blood continued pumping to my legs, and they felt three times their normal size. We all sat on our duffs right there in the middle of the trail for five minutes or so, just long enough to catch a second wind. Or so I thought.

Bill stood up and was ready to move out. Taking his cue, Skylar and I got to our feet. A stiffness ensued, one that felt similar to the aftermath of an intense workout at the gym. It felt as if dead blobs of flesh had replaced my legs and that jagged rocks had replaced the pliable cartilage between my lower vertebrae. I winced in pain that caused my eyes to water. I twisted sharply to the left and back to the right. *Pop, pop, pop* went several of my vertebrae, realigning my back. "Aaah," I let out in relief as the pain subsided.

I asked Bill, "Does Jane still hike these inclines when visiting Gombe?" My legs still felt like numb masses of tissue I had no control of.

"Are you kidding?" he responded, as if I had just committed blasphemy. "She is probably out there searching for chimps as we speak," he added, pointing to the shrouded hillsides surrounding us. I imagined Jane setting out in search of chimps, throwing herself headlong through the thick underbrush in hot pursuit, following them throughout the day, observing as they played, ate, and groomed one another just like a *National Geographic* television special. What was even more impressive was that I now realized the amount of stamina it took for one to trek up and down the hills of this spacious reserve, and she had it. I couldn't even begin to imagine the boundless energy she must have possessed when she landed on Gombe's shore some thirty-three years earlier.

The sun's light warmed all that it touched. Steam rose from the wet earth as the evening's residue evaporated. Turning my head, I caught a glimpse of a beauty that was uniquely Gombe. Illuminated in the distance were lush green ridges like the ones that now surrounded us. The growth was so dense that, had I been light and limber enough, I could have traveled Gombe's landscape just by jumping from treetop to treetop without ever touching the ground. For a moment, I closed my eyes and visualized it. The images in my mind imparted a freedom that was known only by creatures such as birds, butterflies, and chimps. To be able to leap from branch to branch and tree to tree using only the power of one's limbs, or to be able to soar above the trees using only wings, would be bliss. I wondered why God had denied us this remarkable ability if we truly were his finest creations.

Bill's face, which had displayed a contorted expression, suddenly looked as if a light bulb had gone on in his head. He altered our course, and for the first time that day our path began to level off. Our steps became less laborious since we now cut across the incline instead of up it. Leaves continually crunched under our steps, and the trail gradually became wide enough to discontinue hiking in single file, but we didn't. Once more Bill altered our course, and we now began to descend. Skylar and I picked up our pace in order to stay with Bill, and he told us where we were heading. Since our strategy to locate the chimps had failed, we would go to a place where the chimps would locate us, so to speak. Bill was referring to a feeding station that was baited with the ripe smell of bananas. It was about twenty minutes down the path, and he promised that if there were no chimps there, we would have a short rest.

After several slips on the steeply descending trail, we arrived at the feeding station, but to our disappointment there were no chimps. Discouraged but not defeated, Bill plopped himself down on the slanted earth next to a window opening in the feeding station. Behind the metal mesh in the opening sat a man wearing a short-sleeved tan shirt and a green wool beret. At least that's all that was visible within the framing of the small window opening. I believed him to be a Gombe ranger entrusted with preserving the chimps' serene environment. The rangers were armed and patrolled the perimeter of the reserve on the lookout for poachers. Bill and he conversed in Swahili. The guard informed him the chimps had come and gone; they had departed some forty-five minutes earlier, heading north. He pointed his long finger through the wire mesh to reaffirm the direction.

The guard's large, searching eyes focused on me, and he raised his hand and waved. I remember he had a pleasant smile.

Bill remained sitting on the slanted ground and scratched his head in frustration. He appeared like a disheveled scientist in his lab whose work was not going well. A few strands of hair stuck to the slight sweat that had broken on his forehead, while other hairs were wildly out of place. He scratched his head once more. Then his hand slid down to his face. Gently pulling at the hairs in his mustache, he stared pensively into the bush.

The feeding center was constructed from sheet metal, and the walls closed around a cache of bananas that were purposely placed to entice its furry clients. The chimps had learned they could always get a free meal there, and they did so frequently. However, this wasn't the sole reason the center was created. It was also to ensure researchers a spot where the chimps would check in on a regular basis, assuring contact with them while they conducted various research projects.

The feeding station stuck out like a black widow on a piece of white cake. The metal walls were stained in a light, earthy-rust color but it did little to help it blend more readily into the natural surroundings.

Meanwhile, I had my right boot and sock off and was tending to a gigantic blister that had formed on the ball of my foot.

Pressing on the middle of it, I could feel the liquid shift to either side. The words of my father, who was a Marine, filled my head: "Pop it and get hiking." I reached into my pocket for my Swiss Army knife. It was one of the simpler models that had a couple of blades and a sturdy plastic pick; this was what I wanted. Pulling the gray pick from its tiny compartment in the handle, I poked my finger with it to test its suitability for jabbing. Surprised by the sharpness of this plastic pick, I flinched when I pressed it into the tip of my thumb. I thought, "Yep, this will do fine." Before I could give it another thought, I stabbed the honed pick into the squishy mound of skin on my foot and pulled it out. Clear liquid gushed from the tiny puncture, and this release of liquid increased when I applied a steady squeeze to the process. The mound emptied, leaving a piece of sagging skin that no longer fit into that space on my foot. At first there was relief, then quickly after came the stinging that lasted a hell of a lot longer than the relief. I carefully slipped my sock back over my foot, and then my boot. "Ready to move out?" Bill asked, turning to us with his usual smile. We responded in the affirmative and continued our trek.

During the next twenty-five yards or so, the steps I took with my right foot felt as if I had a red-hot ember stuck to it. Soon enough, though, the pain subsided as my body's natural pain-killers kicked in.

The sun was now directly above us, and thin beams of light shot straight down between the gaps in the treetops, illuminating the engulfing forest in a light that appeared supernatural. The three of us approached a tiny ravine bridged by several sturdy tree trunks that had been cut and placed side by side. We carefully proceeded over the man-made bridge, clinging tightly to the railing that was fashioned from small but sturdy branches that had been lashed together with pliable vines, courtesy of the surrounding growth.

Bill continued to cover ground like a machine; the short

break had replenished his seemingly boundless energy. Skylar and I continued to struggle just to keep within twenty yards of his vigorous pace. We were thankful to be on level ground and no longer crawling on wet, slippery soil.

Skylar, reinvigorated, now walked the trail as if she lived there. Her long legs hit a stride that was nearly twice as long as mine. You could almost see the fine, sinewy muscle that lay beneath her Levis. In her powerful movements, I sensed frustration and the urge to no longer hike but run the trail.

Skylar had many talents, and one of them was running. She had begun to run at the age of seven when one Sunday morning she asked her father if she could join him for his morning run. As I recall her telling me the story, he laughed and said, "All right, sweetheart." To her father's astonishment, she did not tire, nor did she distract him with childlike inquiries. No, Skylar just ran, keeping up with her father the entire distance, never growing tired nor fatigued. Once her father realized his daughter was endowed with this wonderful gift, he began training her diligently, and she began competing in open track and field events shortly thereafter. She quickly rose to the top position in her age group for the 400 and 800 meter distances and soon entered events that pitted her against older girls. She did better than expected and by high school was competing and winning regional recognition and was being courted by big-name universities that saw in her that same spark of greatness her father had seen on that bright Sunday morning.

On a sultry Virginia day in August, Skylar visited the college of William and Mary, and it was there she established herself academically and in the world of collegiate athletics. Her freshman year went exceptionally well, and she quickly gained the respect and friendship of the older girls on the varsity team, who immediately recognized her as a running force and a true team asset.

Over the summer after her freshman year, Skylar dramatically sprouted a full four inches and it was this growth spurt that would begin to hinder her running abilities immediately. The following season brought with it injuries and pains that were new to her running career.

There was talk of corrective surgery for her iliotibial band and that became a reality early in her second season. She hoped she would have enough recovery time to still compete. However, a quick recovery never materialized, and the few times she did manage to compete, she lost. Her then unblemished track record soon became pockmarked with losses, forfeits, or alternates.

By the end of her second season, she was forced to a painful realization that her dreams of continuing to compete in college and one day the Olympics was now dashed forever.

I remember Skylar saying, "The hardest thing wasn't letting go of the dream. No, that was the easy part. Where the difficulty came in was making myself stop wondering how far I could have gone when I knew I had the talent to get there." A deep sadness had set in, and we rarely spoke of it afterward.

Chapter Fifteen

I remember hearing a faint rumble off in the distance. The sound grew in volume and ferocity with every step. Bill was too far ahead for us to ask what it was. My brain began to work frantically to decipher the sound. It was familiar, yet I knew I had not heard it previously quite the same way I was hearing it now.

A few more feet and my brain had figured out the sound: a waterfall. As we reached it, we all stood witness to its powerful flow of water. It spewed furiously between two sheer rock walls that extended upwards to a place I could not see since the sun blinded our eyes to it. I squinted, attempting to follow the watery path up to its origins, but to no avail. The steep rock walls closest to the fall were bare and damp and glistened as spears of sunlight shot down upon them, while the rocks farther away grew heavy with brush and green vines that hung in front of them like abundant strands of hair hanging in one's face.

The water collected in a tiny pool, then rushed out over a rocky bed that in turn led to the lake. I had never seen such a sight up close in person, only in images in magazines or on television. Bill prompted us to take a closer look. He motioned for us to continue forward. "Keep going," he said. We looked back at him with uncertain glances. "Go on," he reassured us. We climbed like small children over the smaller, moss-covered rocks that lay about the waterfall's base. The noise was deafening as the roar of water was within an arm's length. A gentle mist filled the immediate air from water pounding atop the rocks in the pool, coating our faces, arms, and clothing with light dew.

The waterfall's strength caused us to take pause and kneel against a slippery rock to admire her beauty and might. Oh, I was sure the waterfall was a girl, for anything this beautiful, gracious, and strong would have to be of the female species. The sheer force of the plunging water looked as if it could drive one into the ground like a nail being driven by a sledgehammer. However, when I reached my hands into the water's path, it was surprisingly gentle, and the water quickly collected into my cupped palms. It was cold, as if it had come from a fridge. It begged to be tasted. I brought my palms to my puckered lips, and the coolness of the water filled my mouth with a purity that could not come from a bottle. At first it was only a cool sensation that I noticed; once swallowed, a sweetness developed that invited me to take another taste. I took a big slurp this time.

I filled my hands once more and turned to Skylar, saying, "You have got to try this." I held my hands toward her as water trickled through the tiny spaces between my fingers, down my wrists to my elbows. She walked cautiously over to where I was standing, almost slipping on the moss-covered surface. I raised my hands once more, this time to her full lips as she sipped the water. It was an amazingly erotic experience. It sent a chill through my body. Small goose bumps appeared on my arms, causing the blonde hairs there to stand on end. Once finished, she pulled back as I stared deeply into her eyes, disappointed my hands were empty. Not realizing what she had done to me, she looked at me inquisitively, trying to figure out what my penetrating glance was saying. "What?" she asked innocently as she ran a slender finger across her mouth to wipe off any spills.

"Nothing," I replied with a sigh. She then reached into the waterfall to fill her own cupped hands, turned, and offered it to me. I drank from her soft hands, and not even the sweetness of the water could mask the sweetness of Skylar. Her hands were now empty; the last of the water ran down the sides of my mouth. Then for some strange reason, I bit her gently on one of her hands. She giggled from the sensation, pulled away quickly, and scampered over the rocks. She glanced back and flashed a mischievous smile that could have melted any man, inviting me to pursue her. A chase quickly ensued, as we climbed over rocks and ran through puddles formed by the mighty waterfall, until I was within grabbing distance. She let out a scream with the initial thought of being caught, then surrendered willingly into my arms.

I turned to sit down on a halfway-dry rock and faced the waterfall. She sat a bit higher up on the rock behind me and wrapped her long legs around me. The air was filled by the thunderous sound of the collapsing water. The atmosphere overwhelmed me with a feeling of contentment as we both enjoyed one of most beautiful places on the face of this ball of dirt we had ever seen. It would've been a sin to not be able to share it with someone special. I was immensely grateful at this moment.

However, the reason Bill had brought us there was not because it was so damn romantic, but because chimps were frequently spotted there. In fact, a few months earlier, while showing a reporter and photographer from *Time* magazine around, they had had an encounter with three large male chimpanzees at the very spot where Skylar and I were sitting. Bill told us that this wasn't a typical observation of the animals eating, playing, and grooming one another. No, these chimps spotted Bill and his guests while perched in a large tree. Shimmying down the weblike tangle of vines, they dropped in on the party suddenly. Weighing roughly 110 pounds each, all of it solid muscle, they appeared ready to launch into a display of authority. Bill told us that just one of these guys would be intimidating enough. But three was damn frightening—especially for his guests, who had never witnessed the aggressive side of a chimpanzee's behavior.

Bill recalled that it was the chimpanzee in the middle, Frodo, that started toward them. "Watch out," Bill warned the photographer, but it was too late. Whack! A powerful, open right hand took a swipe and connected with the photographer's chest, and down he went, the wind knocked from him.

Jumping over the downed man, Frodo started pounding on the ground and throwing handfuls of leaves and dirt into the air. The leaves showered down, adding to the chaotic atmosphere.

Frodo then charged toward the reporter and grabbed his foot, dragging the 195-pound man a good ten yards, as if he were dragging a can on a string. The chimp released him by a fallen tree and stomped off, screeching. "Then Frodo turned his attention towards me," Bill said. He recalled sitting extremely still and being passive so as to not challenge the authority of the rapidly approaching male. Bill got off easy as the chimp just rushed right by, slapping at the ground.

The chimpanzees let out high-pitched screams and visceral grunts that together formed a deafening cacophony as they chased after one another, disappearing into the concealing growth. The two men from *Time* were not hurt, just shaken up with a few scratches, and maybe some damaged confidence, for it truly was like getting beat up with nothing to do but take it.

Bill later overheard the reporter recounting the tale and summing it up as "sheer terror for five minutes." Although Bill disagreed with the reporter's assessment, he admitted it was always a bit frightening when chimps did something unexpected, as they had on that day.

Bill thought the story relevant to our situation since he and the *Time* crew had spent most of their morning looking for chimps and were coming up with similar results: nothing.

Skylar then interrupted. "You mean you're hoping that three male chimps will come down from the trees, hit us, and drag us around on the ground?" she asked sarcastically.

Realizing that what he said did indeed sound that way, he

started to chuckle, and so did I.

Nothing happened, however. That day there wasn't a chimp in sight. Despite the fact that we could hear them in the distance, they eluded us all morning.

I sensed they knew we were looking for them. I told Bill this and added that they were probably watching us from some concealed position, shaking their heads and laughing at our futile attempts. Bill nodded in agreement, and the sincerity in his eyes confirmed to me that he truly believed they were doing just that. I knew the chimpanzees were intelligent and that their genetic makeup differed less than one percent from ours, but to think they knew we were looking for them and that they were eluding us for the pleasure of doing so was almost unfathomable.

"Well, guys," Bill said to us, "What do you think? Should we head back or continue on up to the spot where Jane first observed the chimps of Gombe?" That was probably the most ridiculous question of the entire trip, and Bill knew it, but he wanted to confirm our commitment to the climb.

Skylar looked at Bill. "Press on," she announced. Bill's mouth formed a pleased grin.

Hungry, I pulled out a slice of bread I had placed in my knapsack earlier and ate it. I then tapped Skylar on the shoulder and passed a slice to her. Smiling with thanks, she took the thick slice and ate it, first by nibbling around the edges, working her way around until it was gone. It was the strangest way I had ever seen anyone eat a piece of bread, and it reminded me that there were so many idiosyncrasies uniquely Skylar that I had yet to learn about.

We resumed the upward climb that had started early that morning. Above us in the interconnected sprawl of branches sat two macaque monkeys side by side on nearly the highest branch of a tree. We wouldn't have noticed them, but they dropped something nearby as we passed. Looking up, we saw their long black tails swaying like the pendulum of a clock. They stared at us as we stared back. Their white fur was accented heavily with black. It reminded me of one of my father's pipe cleaners that had been passed through a dirty pipe several times. Suddenly one of them got spooked and took off, jumping quickly to adjacent branches that led to more protective digs. The remaining macaque watched the other scurry off, then turned back to us. A few minutes passed before Skylar left to catch up to Bill. I watched her walk off, then turned back to the astute macaque. There we were, the macaque and I—two inquisitive ones, kindred spirits. Both of us wanted to follow our friends; however, we were plagued by an innate curiosity that kept us both there. Each waited to see what the other would do, but other than an occasional peep, nothing happened. Realizing we were at a stalemate, I smiled and shouted, "See ya," as I left my curious counterpart.

In the early afternoon we finally reached Jane's peak. If Gombe was a church, this perch would be its altar. It held a commanding view. It wasn't so high as to distort the lower valleys and surrounding hills, yet it was high enough for us to see the more distant bluffs that overlooked the limpid blue water of Tanganyika.

Skylar and I planted ourselves on a small patch of ground located where the peak began its long slope downward to the valley floor. The wind had picked up, and fairly strong gusts generated in the east blew into us on a westerly flight path, then went out and over the water. The tall, brown grass that grew at our back gave in to the wind's strength, causing the fine strands to bend and occasionally tap at our shoulders. Skylar frequently pushed back hair that had fallen into her face, but not even the steady gusts could cause her to break her gaze, which remained fixed over the vista before us.

Bill had gone over to a part of the peak that was roughly ten yards from us. I became intrigued with his reaction to the view, which he had probably seen no less than a hundred times. Despite this, he had an expression on his face that told me no matter how many times one came up here, one couldn't help but surrender to its overwhelming beauty. The impact of that beauty upon a person never seemed to diminish. Bill had hinted at this on our ascent, but I assumed he was exaggerating. The twinkle in his eye and the broad smile that swept across his face corrected me. He truly loved coming here, and his love for the peak was infectious and prompted me to soak in as much of this experience as I could hold.

It was here, close to the very spot where Skylar and I were sitting, that Jane had sat for days upon days when first observing the Kasakela chimps. Down in the valley below us was where Jane had first spotted the chimpanzee she named David Greybeard fishing for termites, and as I mentioned before, discrediting the long-held notion that only humans fashioned and used tools in everyday activities. In fact, David Greybeard was important in upending another long-held belief when Jane observed him devouring a baby bush pig. Until that point chimpanzees were thought to be strict vegetarians.

While out on these long excursions, Jane kept a strongbox nearby that she had stocked with raisins and other dried, nonperishable items, along with a blanket to keep her warm when evening approached and the temperature of the night air dipped. On occasion she probably had a visitor who would bring her a thermos of coffee or some food, but as I had learned, Jane was a light eater and could survive on a minimum of nourishment. But there was something much more powerful that had sustained Jane through those early years at Gombe.

As I sat there thinking about Jane, a profound respect for her and all her pioneering work settled upon me. Exposure to the terrain revealed how difficult it must have been to solve the many myths and mysteries that surrounded the chimps. Many thought the work impossible. To begin with, the terrain in which the chimps resided posed many dangers and great physical difficulties. If you were to overcome the initial obstacles, there remained the question as to whether a researcher could make contact without the chimp being frightened or possibly attacking. Then there was the question of how long the researcher could sustain this contact in order to make relevant, reliable observations. Yet despite these daunting uncertainties, Jane accepted Louis Leakey's challenge and returned from Gombe with results that would cause us to reexamine our relation to chimpanzees, forever changing how we viewed them, not only as toolmakers and users but as descendants from common ancestors. This thought helped me to place myself within a line of development and left me wondering how our present human form might evolve in the future.

As if I hadn't already seen enough of nature's beauty, a large bird came gliding into view, far above the tree line. The bird hung there gracefully as it adjusted its wings, using the strong, steady wind to keep itself aloft. It then climbed straight up, exposing its jet-black underside. It steadied itself at a dizzying height for a few seconds, then dove straight down, far into the valley beneath. I could now see the top of its streamlined body and it was a brilliant white that was fringed with the same jet-black shade as its underside. I thought to myself, "Nature is a magnificent painter."

The bird once more caught a gust of wind and shot back up to a lofty height with nothing in the backdrop except for clear sky. I watched as it then rolled slowly to its right and descended again into the cover of flora on the valley floor.

By the time we arrived back at the house, the majority of the day was behind us. We had hiked roughly eight hours over dozens of miles, but unfortunately we had not seen a single chimp. Even though Skylar and I were not disappointed with this outcome, I sensed that Bill was. He knew that the primary reason one visited Gombe was to see Jane's chimpanzees. Although this might have been true, Skylar and I genuinely felt that Bill had managed to show us so many other wonderful sights at Gombe that we really weren't upset. Still, before Bill retired to the house, he left us with a parting thought. "Remember, guys, there is always tomorrow to give it another try."

He then turned and retreated to his room. There he would work on his film project. Bill, through hours of painstaking filming, had managed to capture the live birth of a baby chimpanzee. Remarkably, this had never been done before. As I recall, this initial film project led to him becoming the principal research videographer at the Jane Goodall Institute. I'm sure he was very proud of his accomplishment; however, he was so self-effacing that he never let on to what a big deal it was.

In fact, modesty seemed to be a defining characteristic shared by all who worked with Dr. Goodall in Tanzania. For instance, while at the Dar house, I noticed that several awards had been presented to Jane for her research at Gombe. These awards included the J. Paul Getty Wildlife Conservation Prize and the Schweitzer Medal of the Animal Welfare Institute. Receiving such recognition was, in my eyes, a true benchmark of a successful research career. Yet, notices of the awards hung on a lonely wall in an out-of-the-way place in the upstairs hall.

When I asked Jane why she had not positioned the award letters and the awards themselves in a more conspicuous place, she smiled and asked, "Why would I want to do something like that?" I had no answer. At least, not one good enough to convince her to move the accolades to a more visible spot. A few days later, while alone in Jane's upstairs study, I took a break from my writing and looked around the room, and my eyes fixed upon a poster of two chimpanzees fishing for termites. I got up from my chair and walked downstairs to the foyer, where, on a bleached white wall, hung another poster with the image of a lone chimpanzee gazing toward the camera lens with pleading eyes. I thought back to our conversation about moving the award notifications. It then struck me that it wasn't those pieces of paper bestowed upon Jane that had influenced her to undertake her decades-long study at Gombe. No, her inspiration came from the faces of the chimpanzees themselves, the images of these living, breathing creatures that so closely mimicked our behavior and DNA structure. They were more closely linked to human beings than any other living creature on the face of the earth and to Jane and her colleagues there was no doubt that protecting chimpanzees and learning more about this animal species will ensure the survival of our species - the human race.

• • •

The sound of a whistling teapot woke me to the brisk air of a new morning. The sun was just barely peeking above the horizon, but Bill was already dressed and having breakfast. I nudged Skylar and she groaned as she pulled herself from sleep.

"Is it time already?" she asked in a voice just above a whisper.

"It is," I replied as I kissed her on the cheek and climbed from bed. My throat was dry and scratchy, and when I swallowed, it felt as if I was swallowing a wooden block riddled with splinters. Pain shot from my throat to my right ear. Thanks to the damp, crisp air that had crept so quietly through the screened openings in our room, I had one of those annoying morning sore throats. I labored to cough, and when I finally did, a sharp pain shot once more from my throat to my ear. However, I knew that type of sore throat wouldn't last. No, it seemed to disappear just as quickly as our evening had. The air outside my blanket was cool. The air outside the house was even cooler. The warm, cozy confines of my bed seemed to beg me to stay put. But I knew I would regret not attempting one last try to see the chimpanzees of Gombe. Stiffly I reached out to fold back the warm layers of wool and cotton, and I swear I saw a faint mist appear as the toasty air from underneath my blankets mixed with the cold.

We set out in a different direction from the one we'd taken the previous day. The chimp trail wove through an open area surrounded by acres of knee-high grass that was brown and faded. We entered an area dense with tree and vine growth. Limbs stretched in every direction, interweaving to create a sprawling second story above the wilderness floor.

Suddenly, Bill motioned us to stop and be silent. He mouthed the words "that is Galahad" and pointed up. We stood motionless as above, in the protection of the enveloping growth, perched on a limb, sat Galahad. He steadied himself with his strong left arm by holding onto a branch above his head. In his furry right hand he held a small piece of fruit or vegetable. He calmly ate his breakfast while his eyes scrutinized us just as carefully as our eyes did him.

The coat covering most of Galahad's body was thick and black and possessed a healthy shine. The hair that grew around his mouth and chin was a lighter shade, dark brown. His face was a tawny flesh color similar to our own. Deciding he had eaten enough, he dropped the food on the jungle floor, stretched his legs, and began to move away from us in a drunken fashion. He swayed from side to side as his arms swung in and out of cadence, deftly maneuvering through the narrow branches as they swayed and creaked under his weight. He continued swaying from branch to branch until he came to a place where the branches stopped and the tree trunks formed a forty-five degree angle to the jungle floor—a dead end. Instead of turning back, he sat on his haunches and used his powerful feet to carefully tread down the angled path. Once past the steepest part, he brought his powerful arms into play and shimmied down the trunk to the point where he was able to reach out to another tree trunk. Then back up he went to the continuing trail of branches.

Despite the difficult business of climbing, Galahad managed to pick up something new to eat and now paused to consume his snack. He took large bites of the orange-colored fruit and

chewed them neatly, occasionally puckering his lips and allowing some of the fruit to fall from his mouth. Once finished, he
scratched his furry chest and leaned back for a stretch and a rest
when something above him caught his attention. He reached up
to a thin branch directly overhead and pulled it closer, revealing
a lone piece of fruit hanging from it. Still leaning back, he bent
the branch until the piece of fruit dipped into his waiting mouth.
Chewing the fruit, he stared at us, making a frown-like expression and apparently decided that the morsel tasted bad. He
pushed it from his mouth with his tongue.

We thought he would continue his journey along the
branches, but he just sat there on one branch, continuing to stare
at us with his tongue now slightly protruding from his lips like
a small child sticking his tongue out to strangers. Skylar and I
burst into laughter, and it looked like he was now smiling at our
amusement, as if he had gotten the reaction he wanted. Then,
quickly, he reached for the farthest branch and hoisted himself
higher and higher until he was out of sight. As he journeyed on-
ward, all we could see was the thrashing movement of swaying
branches.

• • •

The African sun beat down unrelentingly upon my bare
shoulders and back.

Exhausted from the day's trek, we sought solace in Tanganyika's contents. Skylar and I sat at the lake's edge as the cool,
therapeutic water rushed over our aching joints and swollen tis-
sues, over and over again. The water was so clear one could see
the bottom, and it appeared that the depth remained no more
than waist-high as far as I could see.

"One more night," Skylar reminded me, interrupting my
thoughts.

"Yeah, I had kind of hoped we wouldn't bring that topic up,"

I told her as I pitched a flat, perfectly oval stone across the pristine surface of the lake. I watched it skip four or five times until the water grabbed hold of it, causing it to sink. The *kerplunk* sound it made seemed to match the sinking feeling in my stomach that Skylar had triggered by bringing up the fact that all of this would end in less than forty-eight hours. We would soon make separate journeys back home to lives that awaited us. I would go back to work at the newspaper in Lafayette, California, and she would head for graduate school in Cambridge, England.

Our trip to Africa had lasted only four weeks, but it seemed like an eternity, and I was so accustomed to life here and being with Skylar that I never wanted to be separated from either.

In Africa, I had grown to love the feeling of never knowing what to expect from one minute to the next. Life seemed to turn over a new leaf here, and what seemed so mundane just six weeks ago was now unpredictable and refreshing. It was similar to when I was sixteen and had just received my driver's license, and had felt the excitement associated with exploring the limits of the areas that surrounded me for the first time without being under the escort of my parents.

Every morning I awoke in Africa wondering what I would see that day, hungering for the emergence of each new experience. I felt a consciousness had been awakened from a long-dormant state. I was alive, in a sense, for the first time in twenty-one years. I realized life was not all about just going through the motions of a familiar and patterned day. No, here life was romantic and dangerous and required courage. Back home, life was bloated with comfort and routine. It was occupied by commuting times, lunch breaks, and a weekend reprieve that usually translated into yard work, dining out, and falling asleep on the couch in front of the television on Sundays.

Out here, life was exhilarating, and it seemed as if time stood still. There was no growing old and nothing was lost. Together we were forever young. We believed in ourselves and had faith in our future together, despite the fact that we had yet to discuss a future together. Moreover, I dreaded being apart from Skylar. Not being able to draw on her strength, share our thoughts, have someone who always understood me—hell, just not being able to bask in her presence caused a sinking feeling in the pit of my stomach. That feeling grew from one akin to a stone sinking to a plunge off a cliff.

There, on the rocky shores of Lake Tanganyika, I sat and wondered what direction my life would take now that Skylar had entered it. I couldn't help but think of what my father had told me years ago. He was sad because his father had just had a heart attack. This had taken him completely by surprise since my grandfather had always been in good health and was only sixty-two years old. Seeing him depressed, I naively offered what any kid of eleven would and told him everything was going to be okay. He turned to me and smiled and gave me a big hug. Still holding me, he said, "Vince, it seems just when you think your life is perfect and all the storms of youth have quieted into tranquility, that's when life feels it has to shake things up all over again and break your heart." At the time, I thought I understood him, but what he forgot to tell me was that life could break your heart with something good just as easily as it could with something bad. Meeting Skylar was one of the best things that had ever happened to me, yet I felt it was tearing me apart inside.

At my feet, I noticed an onrush of ripples. At their center was the place where the rock I threw had landed. It seemed to symbolize my life and how my meeting Skylar had triggered a procession of events that had already changed my life. Just then, Skylar nudged me and pointed to the water. The rays of sunlight had caught the ripples' reflection and created a magnificent, shimmering light that covered the surface of the lake for as far as I could see. I withdrew from thoughts about the future to enjoy the spectacle of the present.

We were both overwhelmed by the beauty of the sunlight upon the water of the lake. Our eyes pored over every inch of it; we were like good detectives at a crime scene, careful to take in every detail and commit it as perfectly as possible to memory. Both of us realized that once we returned home, our memories would be all that we had.

After dinner, we all gathered around in the living room area to drink some Scotch and share some stories. Jane recounted her days of avid chimp watching, telling us about having seen nearly twenty-five chimps, including, as she put it, "the ever violent Frodo," who bristled at her but did not attack. Jane went on to explain that Frodo liked to pick on her, and typically upon their meeting, he would accost her physically by hitting her with powerful swats that often knocked her off her feet. Sometimes he continued his assault and grabbed one of her legs and dragged her along the ground.

The image of one of the chimpanzees routinely selecting her, hitting and dragging her through the forest, was disturbing. To me she was the savior of the Gombe chimpanzees, and to imagine one of them acting violently against her was a shock, something almost unthinkable that left me with an uneasy feeling. Yet Jane didn't seem to hold this abusive behavior against Frodo. No, to the contrary, she seemed to accept it because it helped to remind her that chimpanzees shared many of man's darker characteristics, including insurrection and the most diabolical— warfare.

That evening, Skylar and I again found ourselves on the beach. The sand was still warm from the day's intense heat but was cooling quickly. In the background was the cement block-house alight with kerosene lamps. The conversation of Dr. Jane, Bill, and Charlotte echoed out over the calm water of the lake. We enjoyed one last experience of a star-filled sky unblemished by distracting surface lights. The burning embers packed almost every inch of sky as they cast a seductive light upon our bodies.

Skylar's silhouette filled my sight. I felt my insides swell up like a sponge immersed in water, barely able to contain what it had absorbed. A rush of emotion came over me, beginning in my legs and working its way up my body. Every hair stood on end. Inside my head, what had started out as a faint, simple melody was now increasing in volume and complexity until finally the entire "Blue Danube" was playing in my mind.

I started to chuckle as the melody picked up in rhythm and volume, for I knew immediately why my subconscious had chosen that particular tune. I was recalling a scene from the movie *Goodbye, Mr. Chips* in which the title character meets a lovely young woman while taking a walking tour of Austria. The two happen upon each other accidentally while becoming briefly stranded on a mountain-climbing venture. Immediately upon meeting, they fall in love. However, because Chips is middle-aged and dreadfully afraid of the so-called "modern" woman, and Kathy is much younger, they are both hesitant to trust their initial feelings. So they separate, but as chance would have it, they meet again in Vienna. Both had hoped for the opportunity, yet they are still guarded about their feelings for each other. Finally comes the last evening they will be together because Kathy is set to leave for England the next morning. Chips asks her to dance a waltz to the "Blue Danube." During the course of the dance, as the intoxicating music from the orchestra fills the air and mixes with the dizzying motions of the dance, both are overwhelmed by their feelings. Closer and closer they grow, and as the evening progresses, the tension builds quietly within them as they hint about the inevitable morning departure and their separation. However, rather than letting this burden their evening, they dance on into the early-morning hours. I do not want to spoil the outcome of that particular fictional romance, so I will stop there.

Anyway, that was why the melody happened to be playing in my head and why I had chuckled. For even though we knew that the next afternoon would mean that Skylar and I would separate, we continued to waltz on.

About the Author

Gregg is a native Californian born in San Francisco and a graduate of De La Salle High School, University of California at Berkeley and Oxford University. For the last 14 years he has served as the Director of Development for Court Appointed Special Advocates (CASA) Program of Contra Costa County, a non-profit agency that advocates for abused, neglected and/or abandoned youth in Contra Costa County.

ABOOKS

ALIVE Book Publishing and ALIVE Publishing Group
are imprints of Advanced Publishing LLC,
3200 A Danville Blvd., Suite 204, Alamo, California 94507

Telephone: 925.837.7303 Fax: 925.837.6951
www.alivebookpublishing.com